DATE DUE		
SEP 12 1986	MAY 26 1988	
OCT 16 1986	JUL 5 1990	
NOV 13 1986	OCT 11 1994	
NOV 18 1986		
DEC 18 1986		
JAN 30 1987		
MAR 10 1987		
MAR 28 1987		
APR 11 1987		
APR 23 1987		
SEP 14 1987		
JUN 1 1989		

Miles, Betty
Sink or Swim

oct/86

"This how the Fresh Air work: people in the country say they want a city kid to come visit for two weeks, live in their house like family. Kids in the city sign up to go. . . ."

That's how eleven-year-old B.J. Johnson from New York City happens to be in South Bridgeton, New Hampshire, staying with the Roberts family. He's never been so far from home; he's never picked vegetables from a garden or gone backpacking in the woods; he's never gone to a country fair; he's never been swimming—in fact, he can't swim. And he's never been the only black kid in town. Being in a foreign country couldn't be stranger. But as B.J. recounts his adventures, we realize that he's an explorer at heart, and unsinkable.

Betty Miles has created an unforgettable character in this high-spirited novel. Two weeks in the country with B.J. Johnson is like a breath of fresh air—a vacation not to be missed.

Sink or Swim

BETTY MILES

ALFRED A. KNOPF
NEW YORK

This is a Borzoi Book
Published by Alfred A. Knopf, Inc.

Copyright © 1986 by Betty Miles
Jacket illustration copyright © 1986
by Hodges Soileau
All rights reserved under International
and Pan-American Copyright Conventions.
Published in the United States by
Alfred A. Knopf, Inc., New York, and
simultaneously in Canada by
Random House of Canada Limited, Toronto.
Distributed by Random House, Inc., New York.
Manufactured in the United States of America
1 2 3 4 5 6 7 8 9 10

Library of Congress Cataloging-in-Publication Data
Miles, Betty. Sink or swim.
Summary: An eleven-year-old boy from
New York City goes to New Hampshire on a
Fresh Air program for two weeks and has many
new experiences in a small country town.
[1. Friendship—Fiction. 2. Afro-Americans—
Fiction. 3. New Hampshire—Fiction] I. Title.
PZ7.M594Si 1986 [Fic] 85-23134
ISBN 0-394-85515-9
ISBN 0-394-95515-3 (lib. bdg.)

To all the Fresh Air kids,
and all their families

SINK OR SWIM

1

"You ever see a hog up close?"

This boy next to me, Terrence somebody, been showing off ever since our bus pull out of the Port Authority terminal back in New York City. Bouncing around on the seat, fooling with his lunch bag, pushing over to look out my window. Acting like he a big expert about the country. Just because this his second time with the Fresh Air and my first time. He go to some farm last summer and the people there ask him back. They must be crazy!

"I never see a hog so far," I tell him, "but I bet I see one when you eat lunch!" That ought to shut him up.

But now he rapping on the window. "See that truck out there?" he yell in my ear. "That's the exact same kind of a pickup they got on the farm!" He stomping on my foot, waving his arms over his head to make the truck driver look at him. "You ever ride in a pickup?"

"No." I'm getting sick of this clown. I shove him off me so I can see out my own window.

It feel like we come a long way from New York, but this still not the real country—just roads, buildings, parking lots. Trees, but no green grass fields like Mama been talking about. I like to know how much longer we got to go, but I'm not asking this Terrence. He too full of hisself already. Too bad he have to pick on me to sit down with. I could of sat with that skinny girl across the aisle, except I grab this window seat. I like to see where I'm going. Besides, sit with a girl, she get ideas. Like this girl in my class, Denise— just *look* at her, she think she your girlfriend. Denise crazy! The last day of school, when she hear where I'm going, she make a big scene.

"What you want to go there for? The country *boring*. Nothing to do but sit in a rocking chair, look at the grass."

Leroy, that's my friend, he laugh: "Denise just mad cause her boyfriend going away!"

I laugh too. Back then, going to the country seem like a long way off. Only now, here I am, doing it.

The bus driver hang a louie and old Terrence fall on top of me. He jab his elbow in my chest. "See them mountains out there? That's where we going! Look out, New Hampshire, cause we on our way, coming to stay."

"Push over!" I tell him.

I can't hardly see the mountains, they so far off. I

wonder how long till we get there and I get rid of this boy. I sneak a look at the girl across the aisle. Now she laughing with the girl that did sit there. Having a good time.

I raise up in my seat and look around. This bus is pack! Everybody making noise. One kid in back bring a box. The Fresh Air ladies sitting back there. They from Claremont, New Hampshire, where we going. They come all the way to New York just to ride back up with us. Now they rapping with a bunch of kids. I bet they telling about New Hampshire. I like to hear what they say.

"Where my bag go?" Terrence slide down on the floor and poke around under the seat. He come back up with his shirtfront dirty, wiping his hands on his pants.

"You bring lunch?" He lay his stuff out between us: sandwiches, Twinkies, candy bars, a apple. He pull the tab off his soda and throw it on the floor.

"*Yeah,* I bring lunch." I feel my bag with my foot. I been saving it for later but now he got me hungry. I should be—I eat breakfast at 5:30 A.M. Mama make me eat eggs *and* cereal. But she just drink coffee and talk about the country like she giving a commercial for it.

"It's gonna be so pretty up there! Trees, birds, grass—maybe I better come with you. Kick off my shoes, feel some of that nice soft grass under my feet . . ." She laugh so I know she fooling. No mamas come with Fresh Air kids. I'm not scared to go by myself, but I like Mama to see the country, too. See the grass.

This how the Fresh Air work: people in the country say they want a city kid to come visit for two weeks, live in their house like family. Kids in the city sign up to go. Then the Fresh Air tell you what day you suppose to come to the bus station. When Mama and me get there this morning, it look like half the kids in New York City standing there under the Fresh Air sign. They find my name on a list and a man tell me to go to the Claremont bus. He give me a tag for around my neck. It say *B.J. Johnson,* that's me, and *Mr. and Mrs. Norman Roberts, South Bridgeton, New Hampshire,* that's where I'm going.

"You know they have to be good people," Mama say when she read my tag. "Ask a boy they don't even know to come live in their house . . ." She rub my head. "You show them how nice a city boy behave, okay? Do like they tell you, talk polite, say please and thank you . . ."

"Yeah."

I never go away from Mama before. Even with Mama, I never go anywhere except Coney Island. I been there twice: one time with Mama and my daddy before they break up, and the other time after he move out and Mama and my aunt Vernay that live upstairs take me and my little cousins, Tiffany and Tanisha. That time I get to go on the roller coaster, which my daddy won't let me because he scared of heights. Mama not scared of no heights.

She hug me hard when they call my bus for Claremont, New Hampshire. "I'm gonna miss you, B.J."

"Me too." I stare at one of her silver earrings she always wear. When I be in New Hampshire, Mama be alone. "You better eat supper upstairs," I tell her. "With Vernay and the girls."

"Don't worry about me, hear?" Mama bend down and kiss me. "You know I be fine. All you got to worry about is having yourself a good time up there." She hand me my suitcase she buy for my trip at the Woolworth's on 125th, and give me a little shove over to the line for the Claremont bus . . .

I lay my head back on the bus seat, close my eyes. I see Mama waving, in my mind. She smiling, but she look sad. Then the bus head down the ramp and Mama get smaller and smaller, like a turn-off TV picture, and fade away—

Ow! My head bump against the window. I open my eyes and sneak a look at Terrence, see if he catch me sleeping.

"You know you snore when you sleep?" he say.

"No." I turn away and look out. *Now* we in real country! It look like Out West on TV—big green fields, with little houses out in the middle. Hills, trees . . .

"I guess we almost there," I go.

"Are you kidding?" Terrence laugh. "We got two,

three more hours till we get there, at least." He bite into a Twinkie. The inside splat out on his face. "How come you don't eat?" he ask. "You bus-sick or something?"

"No!" I never hear of no bus-sick, but watching this boy stuff his mouth could make me it. I wonder if he eat up all his candy bars. He could of at least give me one.

"So, who you staying with?" He grab my tag. " 'Mr. and Mrs. Norman Roberts.' " He read fast, like he showing off in school. " 'South Bridgeton, New Hampshire.' I never hear of them."

"I bet they never hear of you, neither." I pull my tag away. This boy making me *mad.*

"They could of," he say quick. "Lots of people in New Hampshire know me. This family where I'm going, the Wheelers? They live near Claremont, but they got relatives all around the state. They all waiting for me to come." He shove a fold-up paper in my face. "Look there."

"Hold still!" I try to read where he show me. *Dear Terrence,* it start out. *Dear Terrence, We are all ex—expec—excited because it's almost time* . . . My teacher give whoever wrote this a F for penmanship.

Terrence jab the paper. "See all the people coming to meet the bus?"

"How can I see, with your fat hand in the way?" He probably think I can't read good. I find one name and read it out: "Bryan Pond. Who that?"

He laugh. "That's no person, dummy—that's where we swim at. Bryant *Pond.*" He take back his letter. "Wait till me and old Buddy Wheeler go jump in that water—" He give me a look. "You ever swim in a pond?"

"Huh-uh." I never swim anywhere. I *can't* swim. Mama was gonna sign me up for lessons at the Y, but we too late so then she say I can learn in the country. She cut off my old jeans for a swimming suit. But I never promise to go in the water. I'm *not,* unless somebody make me. I don't want to go under water and drown.

"There a lot of good ponds in New Hampshire," Terrence say. "Only you got to watch out for snakes and stuff, down under the mud. Turtles. You ever see—?"

"*No!*" Tape his mouth, that's the only way to shut this boy up. I shove over closer to the window. I wish I never come on this stupid bus. Back home, I be hanging out on the stoop with Leroy. Or ducking under the hydrant cooling off or checking out where the Jazzmobile be tonight. Having a good time, instead of riding on a bus that's so noisy you can't even think. There better not be no pond up there. If there is one, I hope Mr. and Mrs. Norman Roberts never go in it. Or their kids. That's something I like to know, do they have any kids.

Terrence jab me in the side. "You got to pee?"

"No." At least, not till he bring it up. Now I do.

How'm I going to hold it in, all the way to New Hampshire?

"Watch my stuff." He jump up. "I'm going back to the rest room."

All right! I didn't know there be a rest room on this bus. I can go there when Terrence come back. I bend down and get my lunch bag off the floor. Now I just want to relax and eat, without him staring at me. I unwrap the sandwiches Mama make me, open my soda can, and lean back. Oh, boy, that taste good! Plus, it so cool to sit and look out at the country. We going past a big forest of trees. I like to walk around in there, under all them trees.

I finish one sandwich and start in on my other one and Terrence still don't come back. Maybe he lock hisself in the toilet. Serve him right for acting so smart. Only, if he stuck in there, how am I gonna go? I raise up and look around. He back there standing in the aisle, talking with the Fresh Air ladies. He can stay there if he want to, let me eat my lunch in peace.

I lay a paper towel across my lap and bend over it to eat my peaches that Mama buy from the truck at the corner of 120th and Lenox. That's the last thing she say, before they call my bus: "Don't forget to use the paper towels when you eat. The folks where you going don't want to see no boy get off the bus with peach stains on his shirt."

I finish my peaches and feel around in the bag for a clean paper towel. Hey, there something down at the bottom—a Mars bar, wrap in a note! The note say *I love you, B.J. Mama.* Nice. I fold it up and put it in my pocket, keep it safe. Then I unwrap my candy bar and eat it.

We coming to big mountains now. The road so high up you can look down on everything—fields, rivers, little towns—just like we a bird flying over. I like Mama to look at this. And Leroy. He suppose to go with the Fresh Air, too, only his aunt that he live with get sick so he have to stay home, help take care of his brother and his two little cousins. Poor him. I'm gonna write him a letter soon as I get to the country, right after I write to Mama. I'm not writing to Denise unless she write me first—and how can she, if she don't know my address? Unless she ask Leroy. She crazy enough to do that.

"Hey, what's your name?"

I look up. Those girls from across the aisle standing by my seat, laughing. They both wearing Fresh Air T-shirts.

"B.J.," I say. "What's yours?"

The one I almost sit with say, Celeste. The other girl say, Sondra.

"What B.J. stand for?" Sondra ask.

"It stand for me." Why tell her? She just laugh.

"Yeah, but what *name* it stand for?" Now Celeste on my case.

I look around. At least Terrence can't hear me. "Baxter Jeremiah," I say, quick. Baxter, that's for my daddy. Jeremiah for my granddaddy, that die before I was born.

"Hey, cool," Celeste say. "Like a rock star name!"

"Right!" I give her a rock star look. Wait till I tell Leroy what she say!

"Where you going to?" Celeste want to know.

I show her my tag. "South Bridgeton."

"Too bad!" Sondra laugh. "Celeste want you to stay in Claremont, like us."

"Shut up, girl!" Celeste poke her.

They both break up. They act crazy, just like Denise. Celeste shove Terrence bag off his seat and plonk herself down. Sondra sit on the arm with her legs in the aisle.

"So—this your first time with the Fresh Air?"

"Yeah." I wish everybody stop asking me that.

"This my second," Sondra says. "Celeste third. We go to the same family. And guess what?" She spit in my ear, she so excited. "Last year, Joyce was pregnant? And she have her baby on *Christmas Day*—"

"A girl!" Celeste yells. "A cute little baby girl, name Sally. Joyce, she the mother, she gonna let us take Sally out in her stroller—"

"Push her all around!" Sondra say. "Show her off! I can't wait!"

"They got a baby where you going?" Celeste ask.

"I don't know." They better not! I don't want to be

stuck with no smelly-diaper baby for two whole weeks.

"Ask Mrs. Anderson." Sondra turn around. One of the Fresh Air ladies coming down the aisle. "Mrs. Anderson!" She point to my head. "This boy want to hear about the people he staying with."

"How come she know that?" I ask.

"Oh, she know everybody," Sondra says. "She, like, the boss of the Fresh Air in New Hampshire. She live in Claremont, but she go all around to see the families, check out if they nice people before she let any Fresh Air kid stay with them."

Mrs. Anderson bend down and smile at me. "What would you like to know?"

I kind of shrug. I like to know so much stuff I can't think what to ask.

"He want to know do they have kids," Celeste say.

"Who are you staying with?" Mrs. Anderson talk funny, like she got a cold.

I hold up my tag so she can read it.

"Oh, you're lucky, B.J.!" she say, real quick. "You're going to like the Robertses, I promise you. They have a boy, Jimmy, just about your age." She look at me. "Eleven?"

"Yeah." She smart to guess right. That's good—a kid my same age. A boy. He better not be stupid, like Terrence. If he cool like Leroy, me and him can have some fun.

"They have a little girl, too," Mrs. Anderson say. "Linda. I think she's about six. A cute little thing, with long pigtails."

I don't care, long as there a boy too.

"The Robertses live on the edge of South Bridgeton," she say. "They have a great big yard, nothing out back of it but fields and woods. And there's a pond a couple of miles down the road." She smile like that good news. "So you can go swimming just about every day."

Uh-oh! I just have to say I don't want to, that's all.

"Are we almost there, Mrs. Anderson?" Sondra ask.

"Almost." Mrs. Anderson check her watch. "We should be getting to Claremont in half an hour or so. I bet you girls can't wait to see the new baby!"

"That's right!" Celeste bounces on the seat. "They bringing her to the bus, Mrs. Anderson. I can't believe I'm gonna see that little baby in half a hour!"

"She's a darling," Mrs. Anderson say. "Biggest brown eyes you ever saw, and cute little curls—"

"I'm gonna brush her hair every day!" Sondra shout. "Buy ribbon in the dime store, make her some little tiny hair bows—"

"Won't that be nice!" Mrs. Anderson smile and walk to the front to talk to the driver. I don't know how he can make out what she say and drive at the same time. I never hear anybody talk like her before. I'm still thinking about what she tell me, about the pond. What am I suppose to do if everybody want to go there? Stay home by myself?

"Push over, girl!" Sondra squeeze herself down in the seat with Celeste so Celeste shove into me.

"Hey!" I shove them back. But I don't care if they both want to sit here. They a lot better than old Terrence. They start telling me what they going to do in Claremont: climb trees, pick flowers, catch bugs in jars. Lay on the grass at night, look at the stars in the sky. They make it sound good. Too bad they not coming to South Bridgeton. Except then Denise be jealous, if she find out.

"Hey, that's my seat!"

We don't even see Terrence till he standing right there. "C'mon," he say. "Move," he tell the girls. "Go back where you suppose to be."

"Don't get excited." Celeste laugh. "We not about to sit here with *you.*" Her and Sondra get up and go back across the aisle. Terrence plunk his fat self down.

I remember I have to *go,* so I climb over him and walk to the back, hanging on to the seats so I don't fall. It's not so noisy back here now. A lot of the kids sleeping. One little boy curl up on the seat with his thumb in his mouth. I feel sorry for him. A little kid like that, gone away from his mama—I bet he scared.

The rest room right over the bus wheels. It's hard to pee with the bus bouncing up and down, but I go. Then I wash my hands and tuck my shirt in. I didn't get no peach juice on it. I hope Mr. and Mrs. Norman Roberts know where they suppose to meet me. They better not forget to come!

I'm just about back to my seat when the bus driver make a sharp turn. I practically fall on Celeste but she don't notice. She looking out the window, yelling. "I see them!"

All of a sudden the whole bus yelling.

"Claremont!"

"We here!"

I climb over Terrence and look out my window. We in a big school parking lot. A crowd of people standing there, waving.

"I see the Wheelers!" Terrence squash on top of me so he can rap on the glass. "Here I am," he yell. "Over here!"

The driver open up the door. The people outside crowd up to the bus, trying to see in.

"Here!" Terrence yell again, stomping on my foot.

"Okay," Mrs. Anderson call from the front. "Nobody come up here till I call out your name. Don't forget your things." She look at her list. "Raymond Adair? Melba Atkins . . ."

Oh, boy, I hope *my* name on there.

Kids start running down the aisle. Terrence down on the floor. "Where my bag? I told you, watch my bag!" He poke around and find it and shove up to the window, waving the bag.

"Hey!" he yell in my ear. "Richard! Ed! Billy!" He going crazy.

"Sondra Otis! Celeste Smith!" Mrs. Anderson call out.

They scream, jump up, and head down the aisle. Celeste look back and wave. "See ya, B.J.!"

Terrence banging on the window. "I see the Wheelers' pickup! You ever ride in a pickup?" He squashing me so I can't hardly breathe.

That's when Mrs. Anderson call my name. "B.J. Johnson!"

"Let me out!" I shove Terrence off me and dive for the aisle.

"Look out for—" he call, but I don't wait to hear for what. I'm running down the aisle.

Mrs. Anderson reach out and stop me. "All set, B.J.?"

"Yeah." I *was*. Only now, all of a sudden, I don't feel like getting off. I look around. That little kid still sitting back there, sucking his thumb. I like to go tell him he be okay.

Mrs. Anderson lean out the door. "Where's the Roberts family?" She give me a little push. "Have a wonderful time, B.J.!"

I can't go back. So I go out.

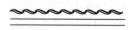

I stop on the top step. The sun so bright I can't hardly see. I feel like everybody looking up at me.

Somebody call, "B.J.!"

I see a man and a lady in front of the crowd, with two kids. They all waving. That must be them. The boy about as big as me. He don't look nothing like Leroy. He white. They all white.

I go down one step. Two steps. I'm staring at this boy. He staring at me.

Then I get off.

2

The lady reach out like she going to hug me, but she don't. She just take my arm and pull me out of the crowd. She tall and thin, with short hair. Wearing jeans and a check shirt.

"Well!" She smile kind of nervous, like a teacher on the first day of school. "So you're B.J."

"Yeah." I wonder if she expect me to look different.

"I'm glad to meet you!" she say. "I'm Jackie Roberts."

Hey, *Jackie*—that's Denise best girlfriend name! Jackie Romero.

"This is Norm," the lady say.

I look up at the man. A big dude with a green cap. He stick out his hand and we shake. He got a strong grip! Strong as my daddy.

"Welcome to New Hampshire." He shove the kids in front of him. "Here's the ones who're all excited about meeting you. This is Jimmy, and this is Linda. Say hi to B.J., kids."

The girl duck behind her father.

The boy say, "Hi." He don't sound that excited.

I say, "Hi." I wonder how long we going to stand there.

People running around, calling out and hugging each other. The bus driver open up the side of the bus and take our stuff out.

"Did you bring a suitcase?" the lady ask me.

"Yeah." I see it in the pile, so I go get it and bring it back.

"That looks like a new one," she say.

"Yeah." I'm glad Mama got me it. Some kids just have paper bags, or beat-up old suitcases, tie with rope.

The man take my suitcase. "Ready?" He start across the grass. The little girl tag after him, hanging on to the suitcase handle. Her pigtails bounce up and down. I never see pigtails long as hers. Some girls I know have corn rows. Denise have corn rows with wood beads that clack when she shake her head. She always shaking her head, to show them off.

The sun so bright it make me dizzy. We walk down the whole row of cars to the very last one—a green Chevrolet. Old. Too bad it's not a new car, or a pickup, but anyway, a Chevy good. My daddy was gonna buy a Chevy one time, only then he didn't. But he know how to fix any car—flat tire, oil leak, battery, all that stuff.

The man put my suitcase inside the trunk and slam it shut. Then he open the door on the driver side and look over the top. "Let's go."

The lady fold down the front seat on her side and the girl and the boy climb in. I look back at the bus. I bet the driver glad he going back home.

"Is there anyone you'd like to say good-bye to?" the lady ask.

I look around. Celeste and Sondra gone. Hey— there old Terrence, way across the parking lot, fooling around on a pickup with a bunch of kids. I don't want to say good-bye to *him*. I see Mrs. Anderson standing by the bus, but she busy talking. "No," I say.

Then a car pull out and I see that little kid from the bus staring out the front window. A lady holding him. He still sucking his thumb.

"Hey!" I wave at him. "So long! See ya!"

He stare at me till the car almost pass by. Then he take his thumb out of his mouth and give a little wave back. He look scared.

I wave till the car turn. Then I get in the Chevy, next to the boy. He look like he want to say something, but he don't.

The lady get in the front and slam the door. "Well!" She turn around. "Isn't this something—we came to town with two kids, and now we're going home with three!"

I don't know if she talking to me, or what. I say, "Yeah."

The boy shove his sister. "Push *over,* Linda."

She shove back. "I *am* over, far as I can go! Mommy—"

The lady give her a look. "There's plenty of room for all three of you back there, Linda. Don't start fighting now, or B.J. might want to turn right around and go home."

Yeah, except, how can I? I'm sign up for two weeks. Two weeks a long time. So far, this not even one *day.*

We get in the line of cars and drive out of the schoolyard, across a big street, and down another street with trees on both sides. Big white houses with green grass yards, just like Mama say.

"Claremont's the big town, B.J." The man look at me in the mirror. "Where we live, South Bridgeton, is just a little place out in the country."

He sound funny, the way he talk. They all talk funny here. I can't exactly explain it. Like they holding rocks in their mouths, trying not to drop them when they say something.

"Have you been to the country before, B.J.?" the lady ask.

"No." I never been to no town like this, neither. It more like a park, with all the trees. We go by more big houses and turn on another street with, like, a castle on the corner.

"That's the courthouse." The lady point. "Over there's the post office, and the new apartment house—" She turn around. "Is that what you live in, B.J., an apartment house?"

"Yeah." I wonder if she think my building have glass doors and a front yard with flowers.

"Daddy, can we go past the store?" the girl ask.

"Sure." The man hang a right.

"Norm works for Grant's Hardware here in Claremont," the lady say. "He took the afternoon off so we could all meet your bus."

"Oh." I hope he not mad about missing work.

"There it is!" The girl lean out the window. "I can see the sign. *G-R-A*—"

The boy—Jimmy—give me a look. "She thinks she can read."

"I *can!*" she say. "I can read *Grant's,* and *Hardware,* and my name—"

Jimmy laugh. "I bet you can't read *rhinoceros,* or *Mississippi!*"

"*Jim.*" The lady give *him* a look.

The man pull over to the curb. "Well, B.J., that's where I work."

The store a whole block long! Big glass windows full of TV's, barbecue sets, stripe umbrellas—man, they must sell just about everything in there. I bet he make good money.

He smile in the mirror. "Well, now, ready to see South Bridgeton?"

I nod my head. I *got* to be ready, cause that's where I'm going, if I want to or not.

We drive on through town. I never see so many big houses. Maybe Sondra and Celeste in one of them houses right now, playing with the little baby. They lucky to go together to a place they know, instead of alone to a new place, like me.

There two gas stations and a Burger King at the end of the town. Then a long, low building with trucks out front.

"That's the feed store," the girl say, "where we get the feed for my chickens."

Hey, *chickens!* Too bad I can't tell Terrence. I bet they don't have no chickens where he goes.

"Want to hear their names?" she ask me. "Sweetie, Princess, Beauty, Charm, and Barbara."

I have to laugh, I can't help it. I never hear of no chicken name Barbara.

The boy laugh too. "See, Barbara's her best friend's name, so Linda named the chicken after her. She's crazy."

"I am not!" Linda yell. "Barbara's a good name!"

"Good for a girl," he say. "But it's a stupid name for a chicken."

The way they argue make me think of my little cousins. They always arguing, till my aunt Vernay make them stop. I wonder did Mama go up to Vernay when she come home. Maybe they talking about me, right now. I bet they be surprise if they see all these trees and mountains. All the little flowers beside the road. I lay my face on the window. I wonder how far we got to go to South Bridgeton.

The lady turn around again. "You're going to be sleeping in Jimmy's room, B.J.," she say. "We set up an extra bed in there for you. I hope you won't mind being kind of crowded."

I shake my head. My room at home crowded too—my bed just about fill it up. But it my own private room. Leroy have to sleep with his brother and his little cousins. Now I have to sleep with this boy. I hope he don't snore. I hope *I* don't. Maybe Terrence just make that up.

"There's the restaurant!" the girl yell.

Norm slow down in front of a silver-color building with a big sign that say Sandy's Dinner.

"Sandy's Diner!" the girl yell. I guess that how you supposed to say it. "See, Jimmy, I can read that, too: *S-A-N—*"

"Okay!" He give me a look, like, she stupid. I bet he can read good.

"That's where I work," the lady say. "I wait tables three nights a week."

"They serve the best pie in the state of New Hampshire," the man say. "You ever eat fresh raspberry pie, B.J.?"

I shake my head.

"Well, we'll have to do something about that."

Maybe he mean we gonna go there. That's cool, go eat where you know the waitress. I bet Sandy's a good restaurant. I bet old Terrence never eat there.

We drive for a long time, up and down little hills, past big forests of trees on both sides of the road. It look nice in there, with the sun shining down through the leaves.

"Hey, B.J.—look," Jimmy say. "We're coming to the pond where we go swimming."

Uh-oh!

"Can we go swimming after we get home, Mommy?" Linda ask.

"No!" the lady say. "Slow down, Linda! We have to get B.J. settled and everything. He's had a long day."

"Want to go swimming tomorrow, B.J.?" Linda ask me.

I shrug my shoulders, like I don't care.

"See?" Jimmy lean over me, pointing out. "That's it. Only we swim over on the other side—"

"Where the beach is," Linda say. "See way over there? *That's* where we go. If you can swim in deep water you can go on that raft."

Oh, man, this pond look bigger than the Hudson River! I hunch up. I know what they going to ask.

The lady ask it. "Do you know how to swim, B.J.?"

"Yeah." It come out kind of funny. I cough.

She look at me, but she don't say nothing.

It take a long time to go past the pond. After it, there a gas station and a couple houses. Then the man slow down.

"Look there, B.J." He point to a sign at the side of the road.

I read the sign: SOUTH BRIDGETON. We here! I

stare out the window. The whole town just a couple streets! We go past a white church with a steeple, a store, a gas station, and a little house with a sign: U.S. POST OFFICE, SOUTH BRIDGETON, N.H.

"Stop at the post office a second." The lady give me a postcard. "This is to tell your mother that you got here okay. Want to sign it yourself?"

"Okay." I take the pen she give me and start to read the card. *Dear Parent, Your child has arrived*—I can't read it all because they waiting. I go to the end and put *Love to Mama, from B.J.* I bet she be glad when she get this.

The lady drop the card in a mailbox. Then we go on down the street.

The girl leaning out her window. "We're almost at our house, B.J. Not this house, not *this* one . . ."

There one house left. That must be it.

"That's it," Jimmy say.

Oh, boy—a big, old yellow house, with a yard all around it. We turn and drive to the back. I try to see everything. Big trees, a flower garden—hey, a *barn.*

The man turn off the engine and we all get out.

"Well, here we are," the man say.

Everybody look at me, like they waiting for me to say something.

"Yeah," I say.

The lady smile. "Let's go inside and show B.J. the house."

The man take my suitcase out of the trunk and we go up the back steps. I guess they forget to lock the door because we walk right in the kitchen. It *big*. Plants hanging at the windows, a table with a blue cloth.

"I bet you're thirsty, B.J." The lady get glasses and pour out orange juice and give it to us. We stand there and drink the juice.

"Well, I bet B.J.'d like to see where he's going to sleep," the lady say when we finish. "Jim, why don't you take him upstairs?"

"Come on." The boy take me out to a hall—I see a big TV in the front room—and we go upstairs. I guess they live on both the floors. Jimmy stop at a door. "This is my room."

I look in. Two beds, and—hey—a *dog* on one of them! A cute brown and white dog, curl up sleeping.

"That's Lucky." Jimmy go pat him. "He's old. Practically all he does is sleep."

I pat the dog too. His fur so *soft*. He wag his tail and look at me. I touch his bare pink stomach. It so cool they have a dog! I like to have one, only Mama say a dog in the city nothing but trouble.

"I hope you don't mind sleeping with him," Jimmy say, "because this is where he always ends up, in my room."

"That's okay." I look around. Two beds, a chest, and a table. A window with a tree outside. A model airplane hanging down from the ceiling. Uh-oh—a

Red Sox pennant! I hate the Red Sox. I'm a Yankee fan.

Linda come to the door. "Want to see my chickens, B.J.?"

"Yeah, let's go," Jimmy say. "I'll show you Wiggles. That's my rabbit."

Oh, man—chickens, a dog, *and* a rabbit!

We go down. The lady peeling potatoes. "Don't go too far, kids. We're going to eat soon."

"Come see my chickens first." Linda pull me down the back steps. She open a door in the barn. "Go on in."

I go in and duck back out again. It *stinks!* The whole room full of chickens, jumping up, flapping their wings and making a racket. Feathers and dust in the air.

Linda grab a chicken and shove it in my face. "This is Barbara."

I jump away. The chicken flap and squawk like it going crazy.

Linda set it down and throw feed on the floor.

The chickens flap around, bobbing and pecking for each little grain. I never see chickens this close, except shut up in cages at the market, or hanging down dead by the feet. Live, free chickens something else. They make me laugh, the way they strut and squawk like they showing off.

"Come on and see Wiggles." Jimmy take me around behind the barn past a, like, wall of stack-up

wood and show me the rabbit cage. "Hey, Wiggles."
He open the door and haul out a big white rabbit.
The rabbit try to scramble up his shirt, looking
around with his little bright eyes. He wiggle all
over—ears, nose, whiskers. No wonder they name
him that.

"Want to hold him?" Jimmy shove him at me.

I step back. "No, that's okay."

Jimmy sit and push Wiggles down on his lap. "Pat
him, anyway. Go on, he won't hurt you."

I reach out and touch the soft fur. I can feel him
breathe—his heart go *plunk plunk* under my hand.
"Hey!" I take my hand away. Some little brown, like,
marbles come out of his ass. "What's *that?*"

Jimmy laugh. "That's just his shit. He does it all
the time."

Boy, I'm never gonna hold him, if he do like that!

Jimmy put Wiggles back in the cage and fill his
dish with rabbit food. Then we go around to see the
garden.

"Those are Mom's flowers." He stop in front of the
flower garden. "She's crazy about flowers."

They look so pretty, all the colors together. Pink,
white, red—I like to pick some, send them to Mama.
She crazy about flowers too. Last week she bring
home a red geranium in a pot, set it out on the fire
escape. First thing every day, she go water that geranium.

"Want to see my flowers, B.J.?" Linda run up. She

point to some yellow ones. "Those are my mari-
golds." She jump around them and squat beside some
green plants. "These are my zinnias. I can't wait till
they bloom—they're supposed to have extra big flowers. Maybe they'll bloom while you're here—see all
the buds on them?"

I nod. A lot of green, that's all I see.

"The vegetables are over there." Jimmy point.

Hey, it's like a real *farm!* Rows and rows of different
kind of plants. Jimmy and Linda show me beans,
peas, cabbage, growing right in the ground. Tall corn
plants in long rows. Hey—corn rows! I bet Denise
laugh when I tell her. Boy, a garden all right—you
want some cabbage, all you have to do is go out the
back door and pick it!

The man come out and call us from the steps.
"Okay, kids—time for supper!"

The kitchen smell good when we go in. There a lot
of dishes on the table. Five chairs.

The lady say, "Jim, show B.J. where to wash up.
But you wash first, so you can pour the milk."

Jimmy take me to a little bathroom under the
steps. We pee. Then he wash his hands and open the
door. "Come on back when you're finished."

I take my time washing up. I scrub my hands and
wash my face with soap. It feel like a year go by since
I wash back home this morning! I'm rinsing my
hands when I see Linda look in the door. I keep on
rinsing till all the soap gone. Then I dry my face on

the towel and hang it up. All that time, Linda just stand there, watching me.

She making me nervous. "What you looking at?"

"Nothing." She bite her pigtail and look at me funny. "I just wanted to see if any color comes off."

Oh, man. I throw her my tough look. "*No,* no color come off. This the color I *am.*" I fold my arms on my chest and face her down. "Didn't you ever see no black person before?"

"Yeah." She look scared. "Lots of times, on TV—"

"Well, this ain't no TV show," I say. "This real life. You better watch what you say, or you gonna get in trouble."

She pull on her pigtail. "Mommy said, when you came we could learn about different people."

"You better learn to be polite, first." I shove out the door past her. Different people! *They* the ones that different, up here. Just look how they talk, like they from a different *country.*

"B.J.?" Linda pull my arm.

"What?" I turn around.

She take a breath, like she getting up her nerve.

"See how tan I am?" She hold her arm out.

I almost laugh. "Look out it don't wash off."

"It won't—" She stop and look at me. Then she kind of smile.

"Come on," I say. "Let's go eat." She just a little kid, that's all. But she better learn not to mess with me.

Jimmy and the man already at the table when we go in.

The lady set down a dish. "There's your place, B.J., over next to Jimmy. I hope you like hot dogs."

"Yeah." I pull out my chair. I *love* hot dogs. My foot kick something when I sit down. Hey—Lucky! He make a little soft growl.

Jimmy look under. "Be quiet, Lucky! He always goes there when we eat," he tell me. "If you drop anything, he'll grab it."

The man look around the table. "Let's say grace."

I duck my head and close my eyes. I smell the hot dogs.

"For what we are about to receive, we thank you, Lord," the man pray. "And we thank you for sending B.J. to stay with us."

When I open my eyes, he smiling at me.

The lady pass out the food. I shake a lot of ketchup on my hot dog and take a bite. Good! They all talk, but I just eat. The lady ask if I want another hot dog, and I take it. Too bad Mama don't hear me say "Thank you."

The lady lay down her fork and look at me. "You know, B.J., you're our first Fresh Air guest, so we want you to feel at home with us. One thing I thought—how about if you call Norm and me by our first names? That seems like the easiest way."

"Okay." I try to say "Okay, Jackie," but it won't come out.

Jimmy clear the table and the lady—Jackie—serve chocolate pudding for dessert. I love chocolate pudding, but all of a sudden I feel like I can't eat no more. I feel funny. I push the dish away. I like to lay my head right down on the table.

"Looks like B.J.'s going to sleep on us," the man say. Norm.

Jackie shove her chair back. "We better get you upstairs, B.J. It's no wonder you're tired, the day you've had." She smile at me. "Riding the bus all the way from New York City, meeting so many new people . . ."

Yeah. I am *beat.*

"You and Jimmy go upstairs with B.J.," Norm tell Jackie. "Linda and I can clean up."

"*I* want—" Linda begin, but Norm give her a look.

"Say good night to B.J.," he tell her. "Sleep good, B.J.," he say to me.

Linda say, "Good night."

I say "Good night" back. Then we go upstairs. Jimmy turn on the water in the bathtub. Me and Jackie unpack my stuff and put it in a drawer. She give me a pair of Jimmy pajamas to sleep in, because it cold at night in the country. I take them back to the bathroom.

Jimmy turn off the water. The tub nice and full. "I'll wait for you back in the room."

"Okay." I shut the door and take off my clothes

and climb in. Oh, boy! I lay back and relax. The water so deep just my knees stick out. All of a sudden, I think of what Mama tell me last night: "Remember, good people come in all colors." I wonder did she know the Roberts be white.

I wash, dry myself on a big towel, and put on Jimmy pajamas. They fit good. Then I scrub the tub clean and go out.

Jimmy lying on one bed, reading. He point to the other bed. "That one's yours."

That the best one—next to the window.

"Ready?" Jackie pull down the sheets and I climb in. Oh, man, this a good, soft bed. The sheets smell like clean fresh air. Hey—Fresh Air! I feel it blowing in through the window, too.

"I'm going downstairs for a while," Jimmy say. "I'll come up later, after you're asleep. See ya, B.J."

"Yeah," I say. "See ya."

Jackie pull the sheet up around my neck. "Comfortable? There's a blanket at the bottom, if you need it in the night." She tap my shoulder. "I'm glad you're here, B.J."

"Yeah." I watch her go to the door and turn off the light.

There still some light so I can see her standing in the doorway, the same way that Mama does at night, looking at me. "Good night," she say. "Sleep well, hon."

I raise up my head from the pillow. "Good night." Then I remember how Mama say to do like they tell me. So I make myself say it again. "Good night, Jackie."

~~~~~~~~~

I can't go to sleep.

I hear them talking downstairs, but I can't make out what they saying. One time when Jackie laugh, she sound like my Mama laughing with the TV. I'm trying not to think about Mama, but I can't help it. If she here now, she come ask if I want a drink of water. I like to have a drink, but I'm not going to the bathroom because they might hear me.

The window curtain keep blowing around, like a white ghost. There some funny noise outside. The trouble with the country, it's so quiet you can hear every little noise, outside and inside. Like right now it sound like something coming up the steps—down the hall—hey, pushing the door open—I scrunch up tight and pull the sheet over my head.

Then, *whump!* The thing jump on top of me. Lucky! He wiggling all over, making snuffle noises.

I sit up and hug him and he lick my face.
"You a good dog, Lucky." I rub his head. "You
want to sleep on my bed?" I push over and make
a place for him beside me. Lucky turn hisself
around a couple of times. Then he flop down,
flap his tail, give a little sigh, and go to sleep.

I close my eyes and rub my toes in his soft fur.
Now I can go to sleep too.

3

When I first wake up, I think Mama turn on a light. Then I open my eyes and see the sun shining in the window. I'm in the country! I look over at Jimmy bed, but he gone. I feel funny, waking up in a new place. I lay there a while, just to get use to it. Then I sit up and pull back the curtain and look out. Green—I like to show Mama all the green grass out there, and the trees, and the way-off mountains. I like to show Leroy, too, and Denise. I wish everybody in New York City could come here and look out this window just one time, see what the country look like.

I put on my clothes and go downstairs. Sun coming in all the windows. I peek in the front room. The TV screen lit up like the set turn on. That's a big color TV. I bet it cost a lot. Plus all the furniture—chairs, couch, pictures on the walls, rugs—boy, there enough good stuff in this house for at least ten apartments!

I like to look around more, only somebody might catch me. I hear Jackie talking in the kitchen. I guess she expect me to just go there. It smell like she making breakfast.

I stand by the door. Jimmy at the table.

"Hi," he say. "Come on and eat."

"Good morning!" Jackie look up. "Did you sleep good, B.J.?"

"Yeah." I pull out a chair and sit down. Uh-oh! I look under the table. "Hey, Lucky."

"He slept on your bed all night," Jimmy say.

"I know." I kind of remember when he jump on me. I rub my foot on his back and his tail start thumping. He sure a friendly dog.

"What do you like for breakfast?" Jackie ask. "Cereal? Toast? How about an egg?"

"Sure. Thanks." I take the cereal box she give me.

"You're welcome." She smile. "Linda's out gathering eggs, so you can have a nice fresh one. Jim, make B.J. some toast."

Hey, cool—a egg right out of a chicken! I bet Terrence never eat one fresh as that.

"Norm went to work a while ago," Jackie say. "This is his early day—he'll be home around three."

"Oh." I pour milk on my cereal. I wish my daddy come home every day, instead of just once in a while for a visit.

"Want to go over to my friend's house, after?" Jimmy ask.

It sound like *he* want to, so I say okay. I rather just hang around here, catch some TV or something.

"I got three eggs!" Linda run in. "Charm and Sweetie and Barbara all laid one. See?" She shove her basket in my face.

"Aaagh!" I duck away. Those eggs *dirty*. They all cover with shit! I try not to gag.

Jackie look at me. "Go scrub them off, Linda." She set a skillet on the stove. "They'll be as clean as store eggs in a minute, B.J., and a whole lot better-tasting. How do you want yours, fried or scrambled?"

I don't want one *no* way, after what I just see. But I say, "Fry, please." Linda better scrub them eggs good!

"We can take my bike." Jimmy bring my toast on a plate. "You and me and Danny, that's my friend, can ride around, maybe go over to the playground."

"Okay." A bike! That's cool. I know how to ride good because this boy in my building, Luis, have a bike. He show me and Leroy how to ride it. If he feeling good, he let us use it sometime. But Mama don't like me to ride in the street, and Luis say not to take his bike to the playground or the old guys that hang out there rip it off. So there no good place to ride.

"Want to see *my* bike, B.J.?" Linda give Jackie a egg.

"Okay." Two bikes—Norm and Jackie must be rich. I watch Jackie crack my egg on the skillet and drop it in. I know what Mama say, she say, when you in the country, you eat what they set in front of you. But I bet Mama don't know what chickens do to eggs.

"Can I come to Danny's with you?" Linda ask.

Jimmy shake his head.

"Why *not?*" She make a face. "Mommy promised we could *both* play with B.J., not just you."

It sound like they plan my whole visit, before I come, like chapters in a book: "What we will learn from B.J."; "How we will play with B.J." I watch Jackie flip my egg. They should of plan "How to not make B.J. throw up."

"Let the boys go by themselves this morning, Linda," Jackie say. "You'll have lots of other times to play with B.J." She set the egg in front of me. "See how that tastes."

I try to check it out. I don't see no dirt on top, but there could be some underneath. Jackie standing there waiting, so I take a big bite of toast and a little tiny bite of egg and chew them together. Hey—it taste good.

"It's good," I go. "Thanks."

"Thank Linda," Jackie say. "The eggs are her department—she takes care of the chickens all by herself."

"Thanks, Linda," I say.

"You're welcome!" She smile nice, but then she start up again. "Mommy, why *can't* I go to Danny's with the boys?"

"Because Jim wants to introduce B.J. to his friends by himself." Jackie turn around. "And I want you to stop whining about it right now. Why don't you call Barbara and see if she wants to go swimming with us this afternoon?"

Swimming!

Jimmy stand up. "Let's go, B.J."

I wipe up my egg with my last bite of toast and take my dishes to the sink. Oh, man. Swimming.

"Look at that!" Jackie smile at me. "It's nice to have *somebody* clean up without me asking."

So then Jimmy and Linda start to clean up too. Jimmy show me how the dishes go in the dishwasher. I like to get Mama a good dishwasher like that. Jimmy put soap powder in and latch the door. *Varoom!* The whole kitchen start to shake, rattle, and roll.

"Sorry about the noise!" Jackie yell. "It's old. Jim, you can ask Danny to come for lunch and go swimming with us, if you want."

She might as well invite the whole *town!* What am I suppose to do, go drown in front of everybody?

Jimmy go in the barn and come out with his bike. I look it over. This bike *bad*—a blue ten-speed. Black seat, silver trim. Man, give me a bike like this I don't care if I can't swim, I just get on my bike and ride around. I lay my hand on the seat. I wonder if Jimmy let me ride it.

He hand the bike over. "Want to ride?"

"Sure!" The seat higher up than Luis bike seat. I get on, pedal fast down the driveway, hang a louie, peel back, and brake hard. Let him know I can handle it.

"You can ride me to Danny's, if you want." He climb on and I swing out in the street. This some slow town—there no cars in the street, and practically no people. One lady sweeping her steps, and a little kid riding a tricycle. We go two blocks and turn on another street.

Jimmy point to a white house halfway down the block. "Stop there."

A red-hair boy with glasses comes out the door just when we ride up. I pull up in front of him. Jimmy get off. "B.J., that's Danny. Danny, this is B.J."

"Hi," we both go. Danny must know about me, because he don't act surprise. "Come on inside," he say.

I lean the bike against a tree and we go around to the back. It look like everybody up here use the back door. A fat lady in a blue apron rolling out pie dough on the kitchen table, and two little red-hair boys poking it with their fingers.

"Mrs. Carlson, this is B.J.," Jimmy say. "B.J., that's Mrs. Carlson and John and Buddy."

The little boys just stare, but Mrs. Carlson wipe her hands on her apron and come right around the table and hug me like she know me.

"Well, here you are!" She stand back to look me

over. "We've all been waiting to meet you! How do you like South Bridgeton, so far? I bet it looks pretty small to you, after New York."

"Yeah," I say. She talk that same funny way like the Roberts, only faster. I can't hardly catch on to what she say till she all done saying it.

"Going to take him to the pond, Jimmy?" she ask. "I bet he'll love that!"

That's what *she* think.

"We're going this afternoon," Jimmy say. "Mom wants to know if Danny can eat lunch over and come with us?"

"That'll be nice." Mrs. Carlson go back to her pie. "Kids around here just about spend their summer at the pond," she say to me.

"Oh." Well, I'm not spending *my* summer drowning in no pond!

"New York City!" Mrs. Carlson slap the pie dough down. "Now there's a place I always wanted to go to, but I never have so far. All I know about the Big Apple's what I see on TV." She laugh. "So I'm glad for the chance to meet a real New Yorker."

"Yeah." She make it sound like I'm smart, just because I come from there.

She spread out the pie dough in a pan. "Danny, you be sure and thank Mrs. Roberts for lunch. And you boys take it easy at the pond. Show B.J. where it's safe and where it's over his head."

Over my head—I don't want no water over my *ankles!*

"Come and visit any time, B.J.," Mrs. Carlson say, when we go to the door.

"Thanks." She a friendly lady. Fat and bouncy like Leroy mama. Leroy mama always want to hug you too.

Danny wheel out his bike. It's old, but there a good basket on the back. He throw his suit and towel in it and we head for the playground. This time Jimmy ride me. The school just a couple blocks off, out in the middle of a field. The building smaller than P.S. 128 where I go, but the playground bigger—like a park, with grass and big shady trees around the asphalt. There four hoops.

"Hey, B.J., want to see where we're going to be next year?" Danny park his bike under a window. "In there—that's the sixth grade." He jump and grab on to the window ledge and haul hisself up. I jump up, too, and look in. Desks and chairs pile in the middle of the room. Look like they painting the walls.

"What grade you going into, the sixth too?" Danny drop back down.

"Yeah." I jump down and lean against the wall next to him. "Six the top grade, in my school."

"You're lucky," Jimmy say. "Our school goes to eighth. And the seventh and eighth graders think they're so great."

"That's how the six grade act, in my school," I say. "But next year, look out cause *we* be the six. Biggest and best, better'n all the rest—that's what this girl in my class say. They some tough girls in my class."

Jimmy laugh. "There's some crazy girls in our class, right, Danny? Like Peggy Holland and them."

"Yeah. Boy-crazy," Danny say. "All they ever do is write notes to the boys."

"Hey," I go, "that's like the girls in my class! This one girl, Denise? She pass me so many notes the teacher get mad at *me!*"

"Is Denise your girlfriend?" Jimmy want to know.

"Nah." I try to act cool. "She just like to think she is." I bet old Denise like this school. She always complain because our school beat-up and dirty. One time in class, she jump right up out of her chair and turn it over to show the teacher. "How'm I suppose to do my work if my chair broke?" So the teacher call the custodian and he bring Denise a new chair from the teacher room. Denise cool. If I get a girlfriend, I pick a girl like her who not afraid to speak out.

Danny look up. "Hey, Jimmy, look who's here."

Two big guys jog across the court dribbling a basketball. They come up and look us over.

"Hey," one of them say.

"Hey," Jimmy say back. "This is B.J. He's staying in my house. B.J., that's Ken and Chris. They're in seventh grade."

"Watch it, Roberts. That's *eighth* grade," the one

call Chris say. "You better start getting used to it, right, Ken?"

Ken say "yeah" the same way they all do up here: "A-yup." Then he tap the ball and jog to the hoop. "C'mon, Chris, let's *go.*"

We watch them toss the ball around. They not so bad for country dudes. This Chris know how to put a move on the other one, but he blow half the easy shots he get. Ken can shoot okay, long as he get his hands on the ball. They keep up a fast rap, like they the big superstars.

Danny laugh. "They think they're so cool, just because they're on the team." We squatting down with our backs against the wall, like me and Leroy do on the playground.

"You know why they made the team?" Jimmy tell me. "Because all the good players are going up to Claremont High next year."

I watch this Chris. He make the same move every time: fake right, hop back, and set up. Let me in there, I bet I slap that ball out of his hands before he catch on.

"Look out!" Jimmy yell.

The ball come at us. We put up our hands. I catch it on the bounce and toss it back to Ken. He wheel, and walk over, eyeballing me.

"You one of those Fresh Air kids?" he ask.

"Yeah." I face him down. He make the Fresh Air sound like some baby thing.

He flop down on the grass. "Take a break, man," he call to Chris. He turn back to me. "I guess it's pretty wild in New York, all the muggers and stuff. Like, people dealing drugs in broad daylight."

Chris come and sit down. "New York City?" He laugh. "You wouldn't catch me walking around down there—I'd be scared some looney would run up and knife me."

Danny look at me. "Did you ever get mugged?"

"Nah." Leroy did, but I'm not saying. He walking down 110th Street and all of a sudden this guy jump out of the park, stick a knife in his side, and tell him to hand over his money. Leroy only have thirty-five cents, so the guy get mad and shove him down and kick him. Then he split. Leroy can't hardly walk home because his leg all bruise, plus his nose bleeding. So now Leroy aunt don't let him go to the park. Only sometimes me and him go anyway.

"New York's a jungle," Chris say. "Like, I read there's some kind of crime there every single second—murder, robbery, rape—"

This guy getting me mad. What he know about it? I bet good things happen in New York every second, too, except nobody keep count.

"Bad things happen here, too," Jimmy say. "Remember when that guy in Manchester shot a gun out his window and killed some lady that was just walking by?"

"There's crime everywhere," Danny say.

Ken kind of laugh. "Yeah, only there's more of it down in New York."

"There's more *people* in New York," Danny say. "So naturally—"

"Yeah," I go.

"You play a lot of hoop down there?" Ken change the subject.

"Some." I don't play that much. I don't have no ball. I use to, but some kid throw it over the playground fence and a truck run over it. Sometimes me and Leroy hang around the playground, and if some dude on the court ask do we want to play, we play. Only half the time the serious players take over the game so there no chance to play anyway.

Chris jump up. "Want to give these guys a game?" he ask Ken. "Them against us?"

"Sure," Ken say. "You kids up for it?"

We look at each other. "Yeah."

We go out on the court. I like to show them, the way they put down New York. Put me down, too, because I come from there. Plus, I bet they think all black people criminals.

We start to play. Chris shoot from the side, way short, and Jimmy get the ball. "B.J.!" He toss it and I catch it. I pass it to Danny but Ken pick it off and score. Then Chris get it down low. I try to block him, but he pivot and sink it. These guys fast. But we cover them good, even if they bigger. Ken miss a long shot and I snatch it and hook it in. One to one.

"All *right!*" Danny yell.

"Eleven baskets win!" Chris grab a rebound, but Jimmy slap it away. He pivot around Ken and jump, but Chris block it. I run up to cover him and he start that same move—fake right, hop back, try to set up—but, hey! I'm in his face. He try a jumper but it way off. Danny get it and drop it in. Jimmy take the ball in, toss it to me and I fake, jump, and shoot in one smooth move. The ball sink through the net. All right!

"Three to one!" Jimmy yell.

They make the next two in a row and even the score, but then we get it together. Dribble, pass, set up, shoot—they can't touch us. Four, five—I take a pass, pivot, fake, and shoot. *"Six!"*

"Way to go, B.J.!" Danny call.

Now we rolling.

Only then Chris grab the ball and hold it. "Look at that." He point at the sky.

At first I think he pulling a move. Then I look up. Oh, man—the sky all dark, like somebody just turn off a light. Big clouds roll up over our heads. Then all of a sudden there a loud *crack!* and a bang like a gun going off.

"Come on, you guys!" Jimmy run for his bike. "Let's get out of here!"

We grab the bikes. I get on behind Jimmy. Chris and Ken halfway across the field, running scared. The wind come up strong and the trees bend down.

Now the sky *black*. There go another crack, and a flash, right over our heads. Then *boom!*

"Hurry up, before it pours!" Danny streak past us.

"Head for my house!" Jimmy pumping hard. The bike bump over the grass.

I hang on the best I can. I don't like this, right out in the open with a thunderstorm over my head. Lightning could come right down and kill me! At least in the city there all the buildings around you. Plus, you can hide out in the subway.

Crack, *boom!*

I yell before I stop myself. Jimmy bump down the curb and wheel out in the street. Uh-oh—a drop hit me on the head. Rain. Hey, it start to pour down like somebody turn on a hydrant over our heads.

"Hurry up!" I yell.

"I *am!*" Jimmy shove the pedals down, and the bike skid through the rain. We, like, drowning in rain! I duck my head and hang on all the way to the house. We push the bike in the barn. Danny shove his in after us. Rain dripping off our clothes. We soak through! We look at each other and start to laugh.

"Anyway, we made it!" Danny wipe his glasses on his wet shirt.

"I bet Chris and Ken are soaked," Jimmy say. "Did you see those guys run?"

"Yeah!" Danny laugh. "Too bad they didn't run like that on the court. But we still would have beat them, because of B.J."

"Yeah. You're good, B.J.," Jimmy say.

"We all play good," I say. "Those guys think they hot, but they not." I like to see them try to play in New York. Put them on any school court, I bet they be too scared to *move*.

Jimmy stick his head out. "Look at it come down!"

We stand in the barn door and watch the rain pouring down like in waves. All the tree leafs turn to their silver undersides. Puddles all the way down the driveway. You can smell the wet dirt.

"It's not letting up. Looks like it's going to rain all afternoon," Jimmy say.

"Yeah," Danny say. "I bet we can't go swimming."

Hey, yeah! I don't care if it rain my whole two weeks. Then we *never* have to go swimming!

~~~~~~~~~~

"This must be our Fresh Air guest!"

The lady in the library jump up from her desk when we go in.

"That's right." Jackie introduce me. She been introducing me all around the town. She say everybody want to meet me, because I'm the first Fresh Air kid that come to South Bridgeton. So far I meet people in the gas station, the post office, on the sidewalk outside the post office, in the

Bridgeton Market and the house next door to the
market where a old man rocking on the porch.
They all talk the same funny way. "A-yup" for
yes, "they-uh" for there. "Faa" for "far"! Plus,
they all want to ask the exact same question.

The librarian shake my hand up and down.
"How do you like our little town so far?"

"It's good." I don't look at Jimmy. I know he
trying not to laugh. He bet me she gonna ask
that, before we come in.

"It must seem pretty quiet, after New York
City," she say. "Aren't you tickled," she ask
Jimmy, "to have a new friend come stay with
you?"

Now I try not to laugh. So far, every single person say that to him.

"Oh, it's wonderful for all of us," Jackie say
quick, before we both break up. "Linda, you go
on and choose your books. Do it quick, now."

"Too bad it had to rain your first day," the librarian tell me. "But we sure needed it for the
crops." Then she throw me a new question. "Do
you like to read, B.J.?"

"Yeah." What else am I gonna say, in a library? I do like to read, only most books too hard
or too boring. Like our school readers the teacher
make us read out loud. I hate to read out loud.
Say one word wrong, everybody laugh like you
stupid.

"Well, Jimmy can show you where the books for your age are," she say. "I know you'll find something you'll like."

"Yeah. Thanks."

But all the books Jimmy show me have little tiny words and no pictures. I rather look at the picture books with Linda. They some good stories in those books. The librarian at my school show me, but I never check one out. Leroy and Denise advance readers—they laugh if they catch me taking out a baby book.

"B.J., did you see these?" Jimmy show me a rack of paperbacks.

Hey, there one with black kids on the cover! They standing on a stoop just like my stoop back home. *The Young Landlords.* I never know kids can be landlords! I like to read this, except the words so small. Plus, they too many pages.

Jimmy grab for it. "Hey, this is about New York City! Take it out, okay? We can both read it. It looks good."

I grab it back. "I'm reading it first. I find it."

The librarian check it out on Jimmy card. "Come back next week, B.J." she say. "We're always glad to have a new customer."

In the car, Linda show me her book. "See, it's about a dinosaur. Want to see me read 'dinosaur'? *D-I-N-O*—"

Who can't read *that?* I shove away and look at

my own book. The kids in the picture look so real, it feel like you can almost hear what they saying.

I never think just to look at a picture could make you homesick. Boy. The country a long, long way from my front stoop.

4

"There's nothing to do!" Linda slide down off the sofa with her book. "I wish this dumb rain would stop."

Jimmy look up. "I wish *you* would stop." He say it quiet, so Jackie can't hear. She getting ready for work. She tell us not to make trouble.

I'm not making no trouble; I'm playing nice. Leroy see all the toys they have, he be jealous: cars, trucks, monsters, astronauts, a whole complete farm set with all the little farm animals. We lay out the farm on the rug, but then Jimmy and Linda start to argue and Jackie come and yell at them and they quit playing.

I rev up a little bike and shove it across the rug at Jimmy. He don't look up. He reading his library book. He can read fast. He already turn a lot of pages. Linda keep turning pages, too, but I know she just looking at the pictures. She can't really read.

She catch me looking at her. "Want to read my book with me?"

"Huh-uh." I'm not reading no baby book. I grab *The Young Landlords* off the table and lay down on the rug and open it. "Chapter One." Too bad the words so small. I never finish all this before I go home. I look back at the cover picture. Three boys and a girl. Whoever paint this can paint good. I bet the story good, too, but I don't know if I want to read it. Why make myself think about New York?

Boy. It feel like I been gone from home a year, not just one day.

I look over at Jimmy. He already finish about half his book! The TV on the table beside him.

"Hey, Jimmy," I go. "Want to watch some TV?"

"Nah." He keep on reading. "Anyway, Mom doesn't like us to watch it in the daytime."

"*Some* days she lets us," Linda say. "Like on snow days."

"That's different," Jimmy say. "That's in the winter."

Winter *or* summer, I have a big TV like that in my house, I turn it on and watch it. Why waste it just *sitting* there?

"B.J., want to make a horse show with all the horses?" Linda ask.

"Okay." I get the motorbike and put the rider on it. "Here I come." I push the bike across the rug. It flip over and knock a horse down.

"Look out!" Linda set it back up. "Anyway, that bike's not in the show."

"Yeah, it is." I put the man back on the bike and

park it by the barn door. "See, this the man that owns all the horses on this farm. Only he live in the city, so he have to ride his bike up here to check them out."

"They're not *his* horses, they're the farm's!" Linda say.

"So? Anyway, he want to ride." I shove the man on a horse and push him down the rug.

Linda crawl after him. "B.J.! Give me my horse!"

"Kids!" Jackie yell from upstairs.

Me and Linda look at each other. "Take your dumb horse." I throw it down. Then I put the man back on his bike and push him across the rug. Boy, she has to argue about every little thing!

I park the bike on the TV table. Like, the man want to see what's on. Pull the switch, turn the volume way down low, I can just check out what kind of picture they get. Anyway, Jackie way upstairs. I pull the switch on.

"Hey, how you work this thing?" I twist the knob around, but no picture come on.

"Look out." Jimmy look up. *"B.J.!"*

Blam—the sound come on full volume! I push the switch back in, fast. A picture come on the screen and fade away again.

"What's going on?" Jackie come to the door in a yellow uniform with a check apron, just like a real waitress. "Linda, did I say you could turn on the TV?"

"*B.J.* turned it on!" she say. "Jimmy *told* him not to—"

"You kids are getting me mad." Jackie pick a pillow off the floor and throw it down on the sofa, hard. "It's bad enough to get to work on time with *two* kids acting up," she say, "much less three!"

I don't say nothing.

"I don't know why I even bothered to take you to the library." She hold her mouth all stiff. "You're not even looking at your books."

"*I* am." Jimmy hold his up.

"All right, *you* are." Jackie take a pocketbook out of the table drawer and slam the drawer back shut. "But you two, Linda and B.J.—you better shape up," she say. "I'm warning you. I don't want to come home after a hard night's work and hear about any more fighting, or there's going to be hell to pay. Understand?"

Linda look scared. Well, she better not tell no stories about me or I shut her mouth good.

"And another thing." Jackie go on. "You kids remember to feed your animals before Dad has to remind you, like he told me he had to the last time. Jimmy and Linda, I'm talking to you. Do you hear me?"

They say, "Yeah."

At least Jackie can't blame me for that. I wasn't even here last week. Last week, if I know Jackie get so mad, I might not even want to come.

"B.J.—" She turn to me. "That's your job, too, while you're here, helping with the pets."

"I know." I don't mind—I like feeding the animals.

"Uh-oh, now I'm going to be late!" Jackie take a comb from her pocketbook and go out to the mirror in the hall.

"You have to help me, too, B.J., not just Jimmy," Linda whisper.

"Well, he's going to help me first," Jimmy say, quick.

"*Mommy!*" Linda jump up. "Tell Jimmy—"

"You kids are driving me *nuts!*" Jackie run back in. "I'm telling you, it's going to be a relief to go serve fifty customers their dinners, instead of listening to you argue!" She throw her comb in her pocketbook and snap it shut. "Just try to behave when I'm gone, will you, *please?*" Then she go out. We hear her walk back to the kitchen.

"So long, Mom," Jimmy call.

"Bye, Mommy," Linda say.

"So long," I say.

"Just *try!*" Jackie yell from the kitchen. We hear the back door slam. Then the car start up outside.

Nobody say anything. Linda suck her pigtail. Jimmy start to read his book.

I pick up my book and turn a couple pages. I wonder will Jackie still be mad when she come home. I shut the book and look at the cover. I guess that kid in front suppose to be the Young Landlord. I like to be the boss of a whole building. Tell everybody the rules: they write on the walls, smash the lights, throw trash on the steps, that's it—I make them get out. Then when only nice people live in the house, I clean it up. Fix the railings, put in new sinks and toilets, fill the holes so no rats can get in. Paint everything bright color. Dig up the sidewalk in front, plant a big tree next to the stoop to make shade in the summer. Plant flowers around the tree, put up a DOGS KEEP OFF sign. They can have dogs in my building, long as no dogs mess where I plant stuff.

A car honk outside.

"Daddy!" Linda jump up.

Jimmy and me run out after her. I wonder if she gonna tell Norm on me, about the TV. About Jackie getting mad.

The back steps wet and water dripping off the trees, but the rain stop. The sky turning bright. The air nice and fresh.

"Hi, kids!" Norm take a grocery bag from the trunk and grab us up in his other arm. "Been having fun? Too bad it had to rain, B.J.'s first day up here."

"Yeah." I stand close to him for a minute. I hope he don't get mad at me.

We go back in the house, talking about the rain and stuff. I guess nobody gonna say nothing to Norm. Unless Jackie tell on us when she come home.

Norm hang up his hat and get a beer from the refrigerator. He take a long drink and set the bottle down on the table. "All *right!*"

That's the same thing *my* daddy say when he drink beer! Sometimes Norm remind me of my daddy. Like, the nice way he smile.

"You like pork chops, B.J.?" he ask.

"Yeah." I love pork chops.

"That's good." Norm take a pack out of his bag. "Because that's what we're having for supper."

Just then Lucky come in the kitchen.

"Hey, Lucky!" I go pat him. "You been sleeping all day?" I practically forget about him.

"That's all he ever does," Linda say. "Sleep and eat."

That remind me what Jackie tell us before. "You want your supper, Lucky?" I get his dish and pour his dog food in it. Lucky start to eat soon as I set it down. He hungry!

"We better go feed the chickens, and Wiggles," I say.

Linda pull me to the door. "Help me with the chickens first." She act like she stop being mad.

The chickens out in a little fence-in place next to the barn. Soon as we come up, they start squawking and cackling and jumping up to the fence, flapping their feathers. They kind of scare me, but I try not to let on.

Linda open the gate and go right in. "Hello,

Sweetie. Hi, Princess, how're you, my little chickens?" They crowd around her like she their mama. She shoo them back inside the chicken coop. I go after her and help her pour out their grain. I can't hardly stand the smell in here. Plus the mess chickens make just about kill you. I bet most people that say "chickenshit" don't know what they talking about. But nobody better say that to me, because now I know.

The chickens calm down when they get their food. Linda show me how they, like, line up to eat. It's amazing how animals act. I got to remember all this stuff so I can tell about it back home.

Then Linda throw some clean hay on the floor.

"Good night, honeys," she say. "See you in the morning." We go out and she latch the door. "Don't you think they're cute, B.J.?"

"Yeah, they nice," I say. *She* cute, the way she act so crazy about them. I bet most little kids be scared to even go *in* a chicken coop.

"B.J., c'mon." Jimmy dragging a new bag of rabbit feed across the barn. "Help me—this thing's heavy." We take it over to a big trash can and dump the feed in. It look like dog food, only smaller.

Wiggles sitting at the cage door, waiting. I feel sorry for him, if he wait there and nobody come.

"You ever forget to feed him?" I ask.

"Nope." Jimmy take Wiggles out. "Here, hold him a second," he say. "A couple of times I almost did," he say, "but then when I started to eat my own supper, I remembered."

"What if you not home for supper?" I pull Wiggles toenails off my shirt. He trying to climb right up me.

"Then Linda feeds him. Or Mom or Dad."

"What if your whole family go away—how would he eat, then?"

"We leave him extra food, if it's just for one day." Jimmy take Wiggles dish out and fill it up from the trash can. "If we go away longer, we have to get Danny or somebody to take care of the animals. But we don't usually go anywhere."

I guess having animals the same as having kids—you got to take care of them every single day, or get somebody else to. Like, Mama take care of my little cousins, if my aunt go out. And my aunt take care of me when Mama and my daddy use to go out. I remember. They always be laughing.

We put Wiggles back in the cage with his food. I watch him eat while Jimmy get his water. He eat one little piece at a time, blinking his eyes and wiggling his nose all the time he crunch it up. He some cute rabbit! Whoever draw Bugs Bunny must not know how a real rabbit look. Wiggles the opposite of Bugs Bunny—soft and quiet instead of loud and crazy. If he my rabbit, I never forget to feed him.

When Wiggles finish, Jimmy put fresh hay in his cage. Then we start to go in.

"Want to pick carrots, B.J.?" Linda come out the door with a basket.

"Okay." I like to see how you do that. I want to learn all this stuff, so I know it my whole life. I go down the path after Linda. The garden all muddy from the rain. I know you not suppose to walk on the plants, but it hard to tell which green stuff *is* plants.

"Here." Linda stop and set her basket down.

I look around. "I don't see no carrots."

"They're under the ground." She grab a handful of some green stuff and pull. Hey—a carrot come up! A big orange carrot, just like in the store, only with mud and little, like, hairs on it.

"Let me do one!" I grab hold of the green stuff and pull, but just a little thin white thing come up in my hand. I look at it. "This no real carrot!"

"It's a baby one," Linda say. "You have to poke around till you can feel the top of a big one under the dirt, and then pull. See?" She hold up another carrot.

I start to feel around. I don't like to get my hands dirty, but I want to find me a carrot. I keep poking around till I feel something hard. Then I grab hold of the top stuff and pull.

"Linda, *look!*" I hold up my carrot. "I find the biggest one!"

The kitchen door slam. "*B.J.—don't move!*" Norm yell. "Stay right there!"

I freeze. Oh, man, what I do now? I look down at

my feet. I don't think I tramp on no plant, but I jump back just in case. I don't know what Norm do if he mad at me. Maybe send me back home—

But he run up to me with a camera in his hand. He just want to take my picture!

"Yay!" I hold my carrot up high. "It's me, B.J., in the country!"

~~~~~~~~

Dear Mama, How are you? I am fine. The country is good. The people are nice. They Jackie and Norm, that's the mother and the father, Jimmy, he 11, same as me, and Linda—

I look up. "How old are you, Linda?"

"Five and almost a half." She look over my shoulder. "Hey, are you putting me in a letter?"

"Yeah. See?" I point where her name is.

"Who're you writing to, your mother?"

"Yeah." I bet Mama like Linda. She like smart little girls.

"Want to tell her about my chickens?"

"Maybe, if there room." I cover my paper so she can't see. I'm not writing down all them chicken names! I look at what I write so far. It's hard to explain the whole country, in just one letter.

I sleep in Jimmy room. (Lucky the dog sleep there too.) They got a rabbit and five chickens! Guess what, we pull carrots right out of the ground and eat them for supper! I am having fun.

I stop. I wonder if Mama having fun, without me.

I miss you. Love from your son, B.J. Johnson.

I put Mama name and address on the envelope, and Jackie tell me how to write my address up here. Hey, I got to send it to Leroy! I find the New Hampshire postcard I buy in the Bridgeton Market. I write:

Dear Leroy,
How are you? The country cool.

I lay my pencil down and figure out how to say the next part.

This is my address: B.J. Johnson, c/o Roberts, S. Bridgeton, N.H. Write to me. *Don't tell Denise!!!*
Your friend, B.J.

I'm surprise—writing back home make me feel more like I'm *here.*

5

I lock the bathroom door, climb on the toilet seat, and check out my cutoffs in the mirror. I wish Mama make them longer. My knees look stupid, and my legs stick out like chicken legs! I jump down. Nobody better laugh at me when we get there, that's all.

We *are* going to the pond. I know we going to, soon as I wake up and see the sun. Then Jackie tell us to get dress in swimming clothes. At least, I'm glad I got cutoffs, not some little shiny bathing suit that show your whole legs. Jimmy got cutoffs too. He say that's what most kids wear to swim in. Well, I'm wearing mine to *not* swim in. I jump down and go back to help Jackie.

"Ready to go?" Jackie fixing lunch to take to the beach. She give me a jar. "Here—you can put on the mayo while I fix the tuna fish."

"Okay."

I dip the knife in the mayonnaise jar and spread a

blob on the bread. Jackie start to chop celery beside me. I like to work at this big counter, with a window to see out of. Except, I have a feeling Jackie want to say something, because she tell me to help her instead of help feed the animals.

She throw celery in the tuna bowl and wipe her hands on her stripe apron. "B.J.—"

"My mother has a apron like that," I say quick, to stop her.

"Does she like to cook too?" Jackie plop some tuna on a piece of bread.

"Yeah." If it's hot out and Mama tired from the subway, maybe she just open a can. But if she feel like it, she can cook good. Fish, fry chicken, ham and greens—all kind of stuff.

Jackie cut a sandwich in half. "I bet you're a big help to your mother."

"I guess." I do dishes and stuff, take out the garbage. Go to the store and the Laundromat. Not that much. Leroy have to cook and do everything, because his aunt always sick.

"Well." Jackie smile. "It's nice how you pitch.in and help, up here. Norm says you loaded the whole dishwasher last night."

"Yeah." Now I bet she gonna say something.

But she just ask, "Does your mother go to work?"

"Yeah. She a secretary." I put mayonnaise on the last bread. That's almost true. She go to this school downtown to study office work—typing, computers, stuff like that—only then the school close because the government cut off the money. So now Mama have to find her own job, without the school to help her like they suppose to. Every day she get dress nice and go downtown looking for work. She fill out a lot of papers, talk to a lot of people but so far nobody hire her. That's why we still on welfare. But I know somebody gonna see how smart my Mama is and give her a good job soon.

Jackie take out the wax paper. "Does your father live near you, B.J.?"

I guess she know he don't live *with* us, cause Mama tell the Fresh Air on the paper she fill out.

"Pretty near," I say. "In the Bronx."

"Do you see him sometimes?" Jackie look like she sad because he not a live-in daddy like Norm.

"Yeah, I see him," I say. She don't have to feel sorry. My daddy nice too. Like, one time he come knocking on our door on Saturday: "Wake up, B.J.! We going to go to the park, rent us a rowboat!" He let me bring Leroy. My dad can row good. He row us around the whole lake. Then we go to a umbrella table and eat hot dogs and Good Humors. Leroy still talk about that time. He don't have a daddy, that he know about. He think my daddy cool. Mama say, never mind no Saturday rowboat, she want a man that provide for his family year-round. She think my daddy don't look hard enough for work. But how she expect him to find a job if she can't find one?

"My daddy a mechanic," I tell Jackie. "Only now he lay off."

"That's hard," Jackie say. "There's lots of folks around here looking for work too. Times are tough all over." She start to put the sandwiches in a basket. "I give thanks every day that Norm and I have good jobs."

"Yeah." I like the way Jackie talk, like you not just a little kid.

She put a carton of orange juice in the basket. Then she grab my arm. *"B.J.* There's something I want to ask you."

Uh-oh! I knew it.

She look me in the eye. "It's about swimming. You know Norm and I are responsible for you while you're here, right?"

I nod my head.

"Responsible to your mother," she say, "and to the Fresh Air program—" She drop my arm and lay her hand on my shoulder. "I couldn't bear for anything bad to happen to you, you know that? I'd never forgive myself."

"Yeah."

She say, "I'm going to ask you a question and I want you to tell me the truth. I don't want to find out the hard way, out at the pond, with you scaring me half to death."

She wait. "Yeah," I go. "I mean, no."

She still waiting. "B.J. *Can you swim?*"

I look at her feet. She have on flip-flops. Pink polish on her toes. I like to say I can swim *some,* but the way she looking at me, I can't.

I say, "No."

"Okay!" She let me go. She smiling. "Now we know where we stand. It's no big deal. If you want to learn how to swim, I can teach you."

I start to say I *don't* want to, but I stop myself. I like to learn, if I don't drown or look stupid. I like to go home and say, "I can swim." Go up to that new pool in the Bronx, near where my daddy live.

I look out and see Linda on the back steps.

"Yeah," I say fast, "I want to learn how." Oh, boy—now I'm in for it.

"Good for you!" Jackie look glad. "It's not hard, honestly. In a couple days you'll be floating, doing the dog paddle . . ."

Dog paddle—I want to swim like a human being!

"Can we go now?" Linda come in. She have a red swimming suit. Her pigtails pin up on her head.

"Soon as you all go to the bathroom," Jackie say. "Go find Lucky, B.J., and put him outside." She call out the door. "Jim! Ready?"

Five minutes later we on our way. Only first we go to pick up Linda friend Barbara. Linda in the front seat, Jimmy and me in back. I look out my window. Jimmy keep talking about swimming, but I don't say nothing.

Linda turn around. "Want to watch me swim when we get there, B.J.? I can swim good!"

"Okay." Even a little kid like her know how to

swim! I bet every single person in the country can, except me.

We go out of town a new way, up a hill. At the top there a white house with a red barn in back of it. Some big animals laying on the grass.

"Hey—*cows!*" I lean over Jimmy. "*Look* at them mothers!" I never see real cows before. I can even see their udders under them—that's the bag where the milk is. I learn about it in school.

One black and white cow come over to the fence, swatting his tail. He some mean-looking animal! I wouldn't like to tangle with him up close.

Jackie honk and a little girl run out to the car.

"Hi, Barbara." Jackie open the door. "That's B.J., in back, who we told you about."

Barbara look in the car. "Hi," she say to me. "Hi, Jimmy. Guess what?" she ask Linda, while Jackie belting her in. "My sister might get a horse! My father took her to look at it last night."

"The lucky duck!" Linda yell. "What color is it?"

"Chestnut, with a white foot. A filly. She might not get it, though."

"Oh, I hope she does," Linda say. "You know what, Barbara? B.J.'s gonna watch me swim when we get to the pond. Right, B.J.?"

"Yeah." I bet you got to go under water to learn. I wonder if there snakes in the pond, like Terrence say. Oh, man, I wish we just keep on driving and never get there.

But Jackie slow down and turn onto a bumpy

road. Linda and Barbara yell, "There's the pond!" And then I see the water, way down through the trees.

Jackie pull into a open space where some other cars park. The girls jump out soon as she open the door and start to run down the path.

"Don't go in till I'm there!" Jackie call after them. She take the lunch basket out of the trunk. "Bring the towels, boys."

We go down the path after her. It's cool and shady under the trees. Then we come out in the sun.

"So, this is it." Jimmy wave his arm. "The pond."

"Yeah." I look around. There a sandy beach with some people on it, and then just water. The water sparkle so bright I have to squint up my eyes to look at it. I can see some kids jumping around, way out. They must be on the raft.

"How about here?" Jackie set her basket down on the sand and we spread out the towels. Jimmy take his shirt off. I take off mine. His chest white, compare to his face and legs.

I look down at my legs. I *hate* my legs. It feel like everybody on the beach staring up at us.

"B.J.!" Linda call. "Look at me!" Her and Barbara jumping around in a rope-off place in the water. That must be the baby place, where little kids go. Plus any dumb body that can't swim.

"C'mon," Jimmy say. "Let's go in."

"Jim." Jackie hold him back. "Wait."

Uh-oh. I look at him.

"B.J. doesn't know how to swim yet," Jackie say. "I'm going to start teaching him, and I'd like you to help."

Jimmy kick the sand. "What if I want to go on the raft?" He look mad.

"You can go later," Jackie say. "But I'd think you'd be glad to help B.J. learn, so he can go out to the raft with you soon." She start down the beach.

We go after her. Jimmy walk slow, like he don't want to be with me. So—I don't want to be at the pond with him, neither. I rather go back to the house, play with Lucky or Wiggles.

I shade my eyes and look out at the water. The raft so far off! The kids on it look like little shadow puppets. I bet I *never* swim that far.

"*Hi*, there!" A big lady on a towel wave at me like I'm a baby. "How're *you?*"

"Oh, hi, Jeanette." Jackie turn around. "Jeanette, this is B.J., from New York, who's staying with us for two weeks. B.J., this is Mrs. Williams."

I say, "Hi."

"Hello, dear." She grab Jimmy's leg. "I bet you're glad to have a little visitor to play with!"

"Yeah." Jimmy dig his toe in the sand.

"And isn't this a *beautiful* day!" Mrs. Williams smile like she invent the weather. "Enjoy your swim, now."

"*Little visitor!*" Jimmy say, when she can't hear.

"Isn't this a bee-yoo-ti-full day, little visitor?" He laugh and duck off. He walk across the rocks like they don't even bother him. The sharp edges kill my feet. Plus, they burning hot from the sun.

"Ow!" I stop and look at my foot.

"What happened?" Jimmy turn around.

"Nothing." A woman staring at me, so I go on. "I just stub my toe."

Jackie head for where the beach curve around. "Over here," she call. She wade right out in the water, up to her waist. She duck under water and come up and wave. "Come on in—it feels great!"

Jimmy wade in. "C'mon, B.J."

I stick my toe in the water. Cold as ice! There gucky mud on the bottom. I wonder if any snakes live down there.

Jimmy dive under with a big splash, come up again, and start to swim. He turn his face from one side to the other like a Olympic swimmer.

I take a couple little steps. The water come up my legs, almost to my knees. I'm getting goose bumps, it's so cold.

Jimmy kick his feet. He showing off. "It's good, once you're in!" he yell.

Jackie waiting for me.

I go in a little more, till the water come over my knees. Up to my shorts. I try and hold myself so it don't come to my chest. Hey—

I slip and reach out, but there nothing to grab on

to. "Hey, help!" I fall in with a big splash. Water squirt up my nose. Aaagh—I come up choking.

Jackie wade over. "Are you okay?"

"Yeah." I'm *scared!* My nose hurt where the water go up it.

"What'd I tell you? It's good, once you're in!" Jimmy laughing.

I spit. He think he so cute.

"Ready to start?" Jackie ask. "The first thing is to lay your face in the water and get used to how it feels."

That's just what I don't want to do! "What if water go up my nose?"

"It won't, if you do like this." Jimmy duck his face under and start to blow bubbles.

"That's right—just keep breathing out," Jackie tell me. "Then the water won't come in."

I lay my forehead on the water.

"Go in more," Jackie say. "Blow out."

I put my whole face in and blow. Then I have to come up and breathe.

"Again," Jackie say.

She want me to pass out? I start to do it fast: breathe, go under, blow out, come up; breathe, go under, blow out, come up; breathe, go under—

"Ow!" I come up and see Jimmy swim off. "You kick me!" I yell.

"Come on," Jackie say. "Don't stop now."

I take a breath and go back under. I hear her say to

open my eyes. I don't like to, but I try it. The water all wavy, with ripples of sun floating down through it. I can make out a big rock on the bottom. Hey, a *fish!* I come up. "I see a fish!"

"Oh, there's lots of them in the pond," Jackie say.

I remember what old Terrence tell me. "There any snakes in this pond?"

"I've never seen one," Jackie say, "all the years I've come here."

Terrence probably just trying to scare me. Or, ha, ha, maybe all the snakes in his pond.

"Now, let's try floating," Jackie say.

Oh, boy. I look out where Jimmy is. I wish you could just jump in the water and swim, like him, without all this stupid stuff first.

"Here's how. Watch." Jackie stretch out flat on the water with her arms in front of her. She hang there for a minute, then she stand up. "That's the dead man's float," she say.

Dead man!

She grab me around the stomach and make me lie flat in the water. "Jim! Come help! Lay flat, B.J. Stretch out and relax. Jim, hold his feet up. That's all there is to it," she say, above my head. "See, you're floating!"

Yeah, but just for a second. The first few times, I have to grab hold of her and stand up. But she make me stretch right out again. It's hard to relax *and* stay up. My legs always want to sink down, even if Jimmy hold them up.

All of a sudden he let go, and I go under! I come up choking. Jimmy waving at the raft. "I see Ken and somebody on the raft," he say. "Can I go out now, Mom?"

Jackie shade her eyes and look. "Okay. But remember, B.J. wants to have fun with you too."

Not if Jackie make him, I don't. Anyway, how *can* I have fun, if I can't swim?

"I won't stay long." Jimmy take off with a big splash.

I watch him go. He swim so good! He make long, easy strokes that pull him through the water fast.

Jackie catch me watching. "Don't worry," she say. "It won't be long till you're out there with him."

She press me out flat again. But now I can't even float right! Soon as I stretch out my arms, my legs go down. The rest of me would go down, too, except for Jackie holding me up.

"Don't let go!" I yell.

"I won't," she say. "But, honestly, you don't need me the way you think. It's the water that's holding you up. People are lighter than water. That's why we can float."

I stretch out again and kick my feet to keep them up. This time I float longer. I even open my eyes a little bit. It's like a whole different world under water, all green and quiet. I see another fish, gliding along like a little rocket ship in space. I feel like a undersea explorer, except I got to come up every time I want to breathe.

"Let's see you try it alone," Jackie say the next time. "When you're stretched out good I'm going to let you go, but I'll be standing right here to catch you."

I start to say *Wait!* but she push me flat. I stretch out and concentrate on my feet. Soon as Jackie let go they sink down, but I kick hard and they come up again. I hear Jackie yell "Good!" Then I breathe in by mistake and swallow a mouthful. Oh, man, I'm sinking! I grab Jackie and pull myself up, spitting out water. It feel like I swallow half the pond.

Jackie slap my back. "You're okay!—and you were floating by yourself, B.J.!"

"Yeah." I shake water out of my ears. My nose and throat hurt all the way down.

"Want to rest a minute?" she ask.

"No." I'm getting it now. I better keep on till I get it right. "I want to do more."

So Jackie help me lay flat, then she let go. I kick hard and stay up. All right!

I do it a couple more times. The next time, I stretch *myself* out on the water, without Jackie helping me. I'm getting it! I'm staying up longer, too. I feel the water kind of holding me up, like Jackie tell me. Like a cushion.

After about ten more times, Jackie say, "I think we better stop—you look kind of beat. How about some lunch?"

"Just one more time." I bend down, stretch way

out, and kick. Blow out, keep on blowing out—hey, this my best float so far!

"Terrific!" Jackie slap my back when I stand up. *"Jim!"* she call to the raft. *"Lunchtime!* You should be proud of yourself, B.J."

"Yeah." I *am* proud of myself. Except, what good is it, if I can't really swim? I look out at the raft. They a lot of kids out there now. Somebody dive off with a splash and start swimming in. Probably Jimmy.

I wade back through the water after Jackie.

"B.J.!" Linda yell from the baby place. "You didn't see me swim!"

"It's lunchtime, girls," Jackie say. "Show B.J. quick, Linda, and then come on out."

"Watch, B.J.!" Linda start to thrash around in the water like she wrestling with it.

I yell, "Good!" If she want to call that swimming, okay, but when I learn I'm doing it right. Like Jimmy.

I can't hardly walk on the rocks now—they feel like hot coals. I jump across them fast as I can. There more people on the beach now.

A little boy look up when I go past.

"Mommy, look at that boy—he's all—"

"Raymond, shush!" She slap her hand over his mouth.

But I know what he start to say. So—too bad on him, if he never see a black kid before. Too bad on everybody at this beach, if all they know is just one kind of people. At least in New York there all kind. In just my one school we have black, Hispanic, Greek, Chinese, Vietnamese, Italian, Filipino—probably more. Plus our principal was born in Canada.

"Hey, B.J.!" Jimmy run up behind me. "Did you see me dive off the raft?"

"Nah." Why give him the satisfaction? I wonder if he see me float. I bet he never look.

Linda and Barbara run up, dripping water, and Jackie give them towels. Then she open the lunch basket. I put my towel over me to keep the sun off and take a tuna fish sandwich.

"Mom, did you see me dive before?" Jimmy ask.

He sure full of hisself! I stare out at the water. I wish Leroy see me float. I bet he never catch on that fast. Leroy hate cold water. He go under the hydrant, I don't care if it's a hundred degrees out, he still get goose bumps all over him.

A dog down the beach chasing after a stick that a girl throw in the water. The dog jump in, catch the stick, and bring it back. Then he drop it and bark till she throw it out again. He fast! Soon as she raise her arm, he in the water, ready to go for it.

"Can Lucky do that?" I ask Jimmy.

"He used to. Now he's too lazy."

"He's not lazy, he's just old," Jackie say. "All he wants to do these days is stay home and sleep."

"We should bring him to the pond, though,"

Linda say. "He could sleep on a towel in the shade. Or play with that other dog. I bet he might go in the water, if he saw the other one do it."

Jackie laugh. "That's all we need, a wet dog in the car with us."

I like to bring him, though. Play with him on the beach.

"Well—looks like you're having a picnic!"

That lady, Mrs. Williams, standing over our towel.

"Sit down, Jeanette," Jackie say. "Have a cup of orange juice."

"That sounds good." Mrs. Williams heave herself down. Jimmy grab his sandwich away just in time, before she squash it. She bend over me. "I saw you out there, having your lesson," she say. "Was this your first time in the water, J.B.?"

Linda giggle. Jimmy choke up.

"It's *B.J.,*" Jackie say, fast. "He did real good— he'll be swimming like a fish in a couple days."

"Did you see *me* swim?" Linda ask.

"Oh, yes, dear." Mrs. Williams pat Linda's head, but she looking at Jackie. "I think it's wonderful, how you took B.J. in, just like family." She smile at me like she have a pain. "What kind of a family do *you* come from, dear?"

I hunch up in my towel. This lady too stupid to care what my mama like, or my daddy, either.

"I'll tell you one thing," Jackie say quick. "His

family sure brought him up to have good manners. You should hear him say please and thank you, and see the way he pitches in with the chores."

"Isn't that nice." Mrs. Williams look at me with that same smile on her face. "I guess the Robertses' big yard is quite a change for you after those hot New York streets."

I crumple up my paper cup in my hand. I like to throw it at her.

"Are you making jam for the fair this year?" Jackie ask. She tell me, "Mrs. Williams is famous for her jam, B.J. Last year she won first prize for her—what was it, Jeanette, strawberry?"

"Strawberry-rhubarb." Mrs. Williams look please with herself. "But I'm making raspberry this year, there's such a big crop coming ripe."

"I know!" Jackie say. "We've got to get out there and pick before they go past."

"Won't that be nice for B.J.!" Mrs. Williams push herself up. "I bet you never went raspberry picking, did you, dear?" She tap me on the head like she my fairy godmother. "Just wait—we'll turn you into a real country boy up here!"

That's what she think! She ain't turning me into nothing. I'm staying the way I am. I like to turn *her* into a big fat pumpkin—*that* shut her up!

"Well, I better round up my kids," she say, with her fat pumpkin face. "It was nice seeing you folks. Meeting your little visitor." I duck away before she pat my head again. "I think the Fresh Air program is just wonderful," she say to Jackie. "Showing these city children a different way of life . . ."

I watch a bug crawl over her big toe. I hope it bite her.

Jackie throwing trash in a bag. "*Help* me, kids, will you?" She sound mad. "See you, Jeanette."

"Can we go back in the water?" Linda ask.

I like to go float some more, get away from everybody. But Jackie say, *"No!* Not after you just ate." She throw a paper cup in the trash bag. "Anyway, it's time to go home." She touch my hand. "Jeanette never did think before she speaks. Don't let her bother you, B.J."

"Did you hear her call you J.B.?" Jimmy laugh. "Little J.B.!"

"Say what?" I jump him so quick I surprise myself, and pin him on the sand with his arm behind his back. "Who you call little?"

"Help!" He still laughing, but he stop when I twist his arm. "B.J.—let *go!*"

I let go. Then we help Jackie pack up, and go to the car. I look back at the water before we get in. I ought to feel good, the way I learn to float so fast. But I don't. I just wish I could swim—show all the people up here what a city kid can do. Show Mrs. Williams.

We take Barbara home and stop at the post office. Jackie come out waving a envelope in the air. "A letter for you, B.J.!"

It's from Mama! I tear it open.

> Dear B.J.,
> How are you? Are you having fun? It's *hot* in New York! I'm glad you up there in the country, where it's nice and cool. This still the same day you and me go to the bus station. But it feel like you been gone a long time.

It feel like a long time to me, too. I stare at the mountains out back of town. I wonder if Mama ever see mountains.

> Tiffany and Tanisha and Vernay say Hi. Leroy been around to ask if you gone for sure. I feel sorry for him, nothing to do but hang out on the street all summer.

Yeah, but at least he *home*. I hope Leroy write me a letter. I don't care if Denise do too. I like to hear what's happening.

> Honey, you be good now. Do like they tell you, and don't forget to brush your teeth. I miss you!
> > Love and kisses from Mama.

Jackie turn in the driveway. "Okay, kids." She open the door. Linda and Jimmy get out, but I don't. I'm looking at my letter, where Mama say, "I miss you!"

I miss *her*. All of a sudden I miss a whole lot of

things: Mama, and my own room, and Leroy on his stoop. I miss music blaring out of some dude's box when he go by. I miss my street and all the people that hang out there. I miss how nobody stare if you black, because they black too.

Jackie look in the window. "You okay, hon?"

"Yeah." I watch Jimmy and Linda hang the towels on the clothesline. After a long time I get out of the car. Hey, there old Lucky, sleeping under the big tree. I go over and rub his stomach with my foot. "You a good old dog, you know that?" I lay down on the grass beside him and he lick my face.

"B.J.—you coming in?" Jimmy call.

"In a minute." I look up at the sky. Little clouds floating across it like fish in the water. Like me, in the pond. I wish Mama see me float! I bet she be proud.

A car turn in the driveway. Norm! I shove Lucky off me and run to meet him.

"Daddy!" Linda start running too.

But I get there first, and Norm grab me up in a hug.

"Hey, Norm, guess what?" It feel good to hang on to him. "Guess what, Norm," I tell him. "I can float!"

~~~~~~~~~~

"Hey, you left your bike outside."

I'm standing at the bedroom window. The

night air nice and cool. A little moth flapping at the screen. "You better go put it away."

"Nah." Jimmy pull on his pajama top. "It's not going to rain tonight."

"So? Somebody could rip it off."

Jimmy laugh. "Nobody's going to rip it off, dummy." He get in bed and pull the sheet over him. "C'mon, get in."

"I am." But I keep on standing there with my head against the screen. It look so peaceful outside, with the kitchen light shining on the grass. I wish I live in a place where if you leave your bike out, nobody come take it and sell it for drugs.

I shove Lucky over so I can get in. "Your folks must be rich," I go.

"How come?" Jimmy sound surprise.

"*You* know." If he don't, I don't know how to tell him. "This house, all the stuff in it—big kitchen, rugs on all the floors, garden, bikes, Lucky, Wiggles, the chickens—"

"Yeah, but that's not *rich.*" Jimmy raise up on his elbow. "My folks are always saying they can't afford stuff."

"Like what?"

"Like, Dad wants a pickup. And Mom wants us to buy more land out back so nobody can ever build there."

"Look how much land you got already!" He take me around the whole property yesterday. It go way back like blocks away from this house. They don't even *use* most of it. "People in New York be glad for just one little piece of all this land you got. They see it, they say you rich, man."

Jimmy don't say nothing. I wonder if he asleep. But then he say, "Still, there's lots of things I'd buy, if I won the lottery."

"Like what?"

"A horse," he say, right away. "That's the first thing I'd get. Then buy some lumber and build it a stall in the barn. Buy a saddle . . ." He flop over on his stomach. "What would you get, if you won the lottery?"

"I don't know." I try to think. "I guess a dog, first." Only, then I have to get a yard for the dog to run around in. And I like to buy a nice house, with a bedroom for Mama so she don't have to sleep on the couch, and a kitchen where sun come in.

I turn my pillow to the cool side and thump it down. "I like a lot of things." A job for Mama and for my daddy . . . They come back to-gether—*that's* what I want the most. But no lottery gonna get me it.

Jimmy make a little snore and flop over.

"Good night," I say, but he don't answer. That's the way he always go to sleep—just roll over and start snoring.

I rub my foot on Lucky back. "Good night, Lucky," I tell him, but he out of it too.

I close my eyes and listen to the moth at the screen. What I wish right now, I wish Mama come in here and kiss me good night.

6

The sheet flap up when I pin it to the line. I like the clean-clothes smell. This my best chore in the country—hanging out the wash. Jimmy and me flip for it and I win. He vacuuming the upstairs. Linda over at Barbara house. I wonder did her sister get that new horse! Boy, I like to jump up on a big old horse, grab the reins, ride across the fields . . .

I pick up a sock that fall on the grass, make a place for it on the line, and carry the empty basket back to the house. Jackie in the kitchen making spaghetti sauce. She like to cook early when it's cool. It's always more cool here than back home. Jimmy think eighty degrees out is hot! I bet he go crazy in a heat wave in New York.

"That sauce smell good," I tell Jackie. I take a pad and pencil out of the drawer and sit down at the table to write. When I wake up, I get the idea to write down every single thing I do on this whole day, so I don't ever forget.

"Going to write to your mom?" Jackie ask.

"No, to myself," I tell her. "I'm writing, like, a diary of this one day in the country."

"That's a good idea!" she say.

The trouble is, I'm behind before I even start. I already been up a long time, and in the country, when you up, you *doing* something. Instead of just lay around and watch TV, like Leroy probably doing now. That's all he ever do when he get up, is watch TV.

I take my pencil and start to write.

A DAY IN THE COUNTRY

by B.J. Johnson

7:30 A.M. Wake up. Lucky (the dog) got to go out. I put him out. Norm and Jackie (the father and mother) eating breakfast in the kitchen. They say, "Good morning, B.J." I say, "Good morning." Norm say, "Well, I am going to go to work now, see you all later." He go out. Lucky come back in. Linda (the girl) come downstairs. Jackie start to brush her hair.

I go upstairs and tell Jimmy (my friend), "Wake up!" But he don't. So I get a cup of water and throw it on his face. Then he jump up! He curse. I laugh. He grab my cup and pour the rest of the water on my head. Then he laugh. We get dress and go downstairs.

8:00 A.M. Eat breakfast. I eat: 2 eggs (fresh), toast,

peach jam, milk, and orange juice. Jimmy ask: "You want to call Danny (our friend) and go out back to the tree house?" I say, "Sure." Jackie say, "You boys are not going any place until you clean up your room, it is a mess. Plus, don't forget your other chores."

8:30 A.M. Do chores. 1. Feed Wiggles (rabbit). His cage getting old. Me and Jimmy going to build him a new cage. 2. Feed chickens (5). I find three eggs! I take them inside and wash off the s--t. 3. Clean the room: make the beds and sweep the floor. Lucky come and jump on my bed. Jimmy say, "I bet he thinks we cleaned up the room for him!" 4. I hang out the wash. Then I come in the kitchen and start to write this.

"What's that?" Jimmy look over my shoulder.

I show him.

"Hey, cool," he say.

"Yeah," I say, "except it's too long. Look how much I write, and I'm only up to now!"

He laugh. "And if you sit here and write all day, you can't go do any stuff to write *about.*" He look up. "Anyway, here's Danny, so you have to stop. Mom, can we make sandwiches to take to the tree house?"

"Sure," Jackie say. "There's some cheese and maybe some baloney. Or peanut butter and jelly. Take some apples, too, if you want."

9:20 A.M. Danny come over to go to the tree house. We make sandwiches to take. Baloney, cheese, peanut butter and jelly. We take apples, too.

"B.J., come *on!* We're never gonna get there if you keep writing."

"I'm coming." I look at the clock. "Just let me put one thing."

10:10 A.M. Go to tree house.

1:30 P.M. Come back from tree house. It's high up in a pine tree. You have to climb up there on a ladder nail to the trunk. Some steps broke. It's hard to climb up. From up there South Bridgeton look like a painting in a museum.

Danny know all about birds. We see a kingfisher, two cedar waxwings, and a bunch of yellow warblers. We hear a thrush sing but we don't see it. I tell Danny about the men that keep pigeons in coops on roofs in New York, which he never hear about before.

I get 8 mosquito bites at the tree house. They itch!

2:00 P.M. Go to pond.

4:30 P.M. Come home from the pond. I float and kick from the beach to the rope and back! Jackie say, "You did good, B.J. I know you will swim to the raft soon."

I don't know.

"I bet you could practically swim right now," Jimmy say. We hanging out in the front room before supper.

"How do you know what I can do? You out on the raft the whole time!"

Him and Danny. This girl from their class, Peggy

Holland, that come back from Girl Scout camp, she out there too. She can dive good.

"Well, at least you're not scared of the water," Jimmy say, "like I used to be." He give me a look like he daring me to laugh. "I didn't learn how to swim till I was nine years old."

"So? I'm *eleven.*"

"Yeah, but you don't live near a pond that all your friends can swim in and you can't."

I'm surprise—he swim so good, I can't believe he ever scared of the water.

"Don't tell anybody I told you," he say.

"I won't," I say.

Jackie come to the door. "Boys, go pick some salad stuff for supper, please."

5:00 P.M. Go pick vegetables.

"Bring some zucchini too," Jackie tell us, when we go out.

"We just had zucchini!" Jimmy say. "I'm getting tired of it."

"You better not get tired of it," Jackie come back, quick. "You're going to eat a lot more before summer's over."

I don't mind zucchini, except it's kind of boring. What I'm waiting for is corn. Jimmy say it's almost ripe. You can tell because the silk on the ears turning dark. I squat down by a row of zucchini and reach in under a big prickly leaf. "Hey—*look* at all the little squashes in there!"

"Yeah—and all the squash flowers are just going to turn into more of them." Jimmy hold up a big squash. "How about this one that Dad missed!"

Last night Norm throw six monster zucchinis on the compost—that's a pile of, like, plant trash. When it rot it make fertilizer for the garden, so it's not a waste to throw the stuff there. Big zucchinis don't taste so good. It's better to pick them off and let the plant grow new little ones. But I still don't like it when Norm throw them away. I bet lots of people in New York be glad for the squash that's rotting on our compost. Plus all the apples that fall off trees by the road. I like to pick them up, send them home, and give them away free to hungry people.

5:20 P.M. Feed the pets.

6:00 P.M. I am writing this at the table but now I have to set the table. I will write more later.

10:30 P.M. I am writing this in bed because I did not have time before.

Back to 6:30 P.M. Eat supper. Norm say he going to take me and Jimmy camping! We going to hike in the woods, cook on a campfire, and sleep out in a tent! I can't wait!! Norm say Linda can't come because she too little. Linda cry.

7:30 P.M. Me and Jimmy and Linda play Kick the Can with Danny and his little brothers. It's cool to play out in the night and nobody bother you—except the mosquitoes. I get 3 more bites.

9:00 P.M. Come home. Linda ask, "Do you want to read my book?" I say, "Okay." It's a good story called *Danny and the Dinosaur*. I read her the whole book! Linda say, "Thank you, B.J."

Then Norm read *The Young Landlords*. He reading us one chapter every night. He start to read it out loud because me and Jimmy both want to read the book. Now we can all hear it. He read a funny part where Paul get stuck in the bathroom with a girl, Gloria. We all laughing.

10:00 P.M. Linda go to bed.

10:30 P.M. Jimmy and me go up.

10:45 P.M. Jackie call, "Boys! Turn off your light!" I got to stop writing. I write five whole pages in one day!!!

THE END

I like to write about the crickets but it take too long to explain. I shove my diary under my pillow. Jimmy teach me how to tell the temperature by cricket chirps: count the number of chirps in 14 seconds and add 40. That's the temperature. We try it two nights and it work.

Jackie come to the door. "Good night, kids. Don't stay awake talking like you did last night. Okay? You need your sleep."

We say okay.

Jackie go out.

I close my eyes and listen to the crickets. "I can't wait to go camping!" I whisper to Jimmy.

"Me, either." He roll over. "You know why Dad won't let Linda come? Because she's a baby. This one night, before you came, her and Barbara fixed up a tent in the backyard, but soon as it got dark they dragged all their stuff back in. They said the mosquitoes were biting them, but I know they were just scared of the dark."

I open my eyes and look at the sky out my window. *I'm* not gonna be scared of the dark. What can happen, if Norm right there? I just hope no wild animals come around. I pull the blanket up to my neck.

"Maybe they think a wild animal get them," I say.

"In the backyard?" He laugh. "In the woods, that's different. There's lots of animals out in the woods— deer, raccoon, porcupine, maybe even bears."

"Bears?"

"Well, probably not where we're going. But you want to hear something?" Jimmy sit up. "Last year, up near Gorham, this family was camping out? And in the night, they heard a noise outside and they peeked out of their tent and there was a big bear, poking his nose in their garbage pail! I read about it in the paper."

Oh, man! If I look out my tent and see a bear I probably pass out. *Die!* "How far is Gorham from here?" I ask.

Jimmy slide back down in his bed. "A long way. Anyway, don't worry." He thump his pillow. "Dad says bears are more scared of people than people are of bears. He says if you don't bother a bear, it won't bother you."

"Yeah." I'm not planning to bother no bear, that for sure! But I just as soon not see one, neither.

⁓⁓⁓⁓⁓⁓

"Hey, B.J.!" Linda yell. "Look what I can do!"

I act like I don't hear. I'm sick of looking every time she poke her head in the water.

"B.J.!"

I keep on wading out. Let her find somebody else to show off to. She Jimmy sister, not mine— let him come in off the raft and look at her. Jackie watch, but she way back there on her towel. She stop coming in with me—she say I got to practice by myself. So how *can* I practice, if Linda keep pestering me? Anyway, it's boring to just stand in the shallow water and do strokes. Jimmy always head for the raft, soon as he come. Jackie say, "Stay with B.J. a while," but I tell him, "Go on out to the raft." Hang around here, he just bother me.

I turn around, check that Jackie can see me.

She wave. I squat down in the water, get myself wet slow. Then I lay my face down in and start to breathe in time with my arm strokes, like Jackie show me.

Arm out, face up, breathe in. Arm out, face down, breathe out. Arm, face, breathe. Arm, face, breathe—do it a lot of times, you get the feel of it. I make myself do it ten times, twenty. Thirty. Then I walk out deeper and stretch out and float, just to relax myself. I like to lay on top of the water and look down under like I'm the king of the water world. I kick my feet and shoot ahead. Hey, if I could just keep doing that—breathe, kick . . . Hey, yeah—stroke, breathe, kick, stroke, breathe, kick—I'm doing it! I'm practically swim—

Aaagh! Water come up my nose and I choke. I reach my foot down. I can't touch bottom!

Oh, man, I'm going under! I can't breathe— I'm drowning! Somebody help me! I got to breathe! Got to head for the light. I kick hard, reach out my arms, and pull myself up and up through the water. Kick, stroke—*hey,* I'm swimming! I go till my feet hit bottom, and I stand up, choking and coughing so I can't hardly catch my breath. My nose sting way back to my throat. Water in my eyes, my ears . . . . But I don't care, because—

"B.J.! *Look at me!*" Linda waving like nothing even happen.

I spit, wipe my face, and shake the water out of my ears. Then I wave back.

"Linda! Want to see me swim?"

7

"Oh, B.J., you're going to have to change." Jackie look me over. "Go out dressed like that, you'll come home all covered with scratches. You need long pants, a long-sleeve shirt—put on some socks, too."

"Okay." She talk like we going on a dangerous mission, instead of just out to pick berries. Raspberries. I never taste any, that I know of. Raspberry Kool-Aid, but that don't count—all Kool-Aid taste the same to me. But raspberries got to be good, the way people up here talk about them. "Get your raspberries yet?" That's the first thing they say, after they done talking about the weather.

Linda run in the kitchen. "I'm ready." She look like a stuff rag doll, with her stripe overalls and two shirts and a bandanna on her head. Cute.

Jimmy sitting on the bed when I go up, tying his shoes. He have on long pants.

I look around for my pants. There nothing on the

floor except Lucky. "Hey," I go, "you see my jeans anywhere?"

"The ones with mud all over them? I threw them in the wash."

"What am I suppose to wear, then? Jackie say wear long pants."

"Wear some other pair."

"I don't *have* no other pair, dummy." My other pair what Mama made cutoffs from.

"So, wear some of mine." Jimmy look in a drawer and pull out some jeans. He got more clothes in that chest than me and Leroy put together. Plus, his closet full of more clothes.

I put on his jeans and my own long-sleeve T-shirt. "C'mon, let's go."

"Wait." Jimmy hunt around in his drawer and take out a Red Sox hat. "Keep the sun off me." He slap it on his head.

"I rather burn up, than wear a Red Sox hat." I laugh. "Wear that hat in New York City, you *dead,* man."

"Yeah, well, I wouldn't wear a *Yankee* hat if the sun was blinding me." He come back fast, for a country kid.

I'm faster. "You *already* blind, cause you can't see the Red Sox the worse team in the league!"

"Oh, yeah?" He looking around in the closet. "You want to wear this?" He bring out a hat.

"Hey, yeah." It's a green hat like Norm wear, with

GRANT'S HARDWARE on the front. I put it on and
sneak a look in the mirror. Cool. I pull the front down
low like Norm. "C'mon." I pat Lucky good-bye and
we go downstairs.

"Hey, B.J." Jackie look up. "That's a good-looking
hat!"

"I loaned it to him," Jimmy say. "The jeans, too,
cause his are in the wash."

Jackie pull my hat straight. "We have to make
time to go to town," she say. "Show you around
Grant's, do some shopping—it's time to buy school
clothes." She look at me kind of careful. "I'd like to
get you some things for school, B.J., if it's okay."

"Sure." I don't care if she want to buy me something, like a present. But I got to get her a present
back. Her and Norm. And Jimmy. Linda—oh, man,
and I got to bring Mama a present, and Leroy.
How'm I gonna do all that?

"Where are we going?" Linda ask. "Up to the old
house?"

Jackie nod. "There's always the most berries up
there. Anyway, B.J.'d like to see it."

Me and Jimmy race to the car and I win. I get in
back. Jimmy get in after me.

"Jimmy always gets to sit with B.J." Linda climb
in the front.

"I thought you liked the front," he say.

"I do, but I like to sit next to B.J., too." She yank
her seat belt down. "It's no fair! You get to do every-

thing with B.J. Sleep in the same room, talk half the night—you should hear them, Mommy, they talk so loud I can't go to sleep."

"Yeah, I've heard some of that." Jackie give us a look in the mirror. "Last night, I couldn't believe it. Norm looked at his watch, it was almost midnight, and you two were still going at it up there. I'm surprised you manage to get out of bed in the morning."

Jimmy kick me. We try not to laugh. I didn't think they hear us from downstairs! We got to talk more quiet.

Jackie make a turn before we come to the pond road. I'm getting to know all the roads around here. Most of the time there no real signs. You have to make up your own signs to remind you, like a mailbox, or a big tree or a fence. I know I never see the road we on now.

"The fairground is on this road," Jimmy say, looking out. "I'll show you, in a minute. There!" He point to a big field with a kind of low barn on it. "That's where they have the exhibits."

"I can't wait for the fair!" Linda turn around. "B.J., will you come watch the animal show?"

"Sure," I tell her. "Me and Jimmy both—we gonna come root for Sweetie." She training Sweetie to follow her around, just like a little dog.

Jackie say, "That's something good you get to do with B.J., Linda—go to the fair. I'm glad it's going to be on while you're still here, B.J." She staring at me funny in the mirror. "These two weeks are just flying by," she say. "There's so many things we want to do before you leave, and you'll be going home before we know it."

"Yeah," I look away. Before she say that, going home seem far off. Now, all of a sudden, it don't.

"Why can't B.J. stay here longer?" Linda ask.

"Yeah," Jimmy say. "At least till school starts."

I might not mind.

But Jackie say, "No, that's all been arranged. When we signed up with the Fresh Air program last winter, we agreed to the two weeks." She look at me again. "Anyway, your mom wouldn't like it if we kept you longer, B.J. I bet she's already counting the days till you come home."

Yeah. I hope Mama get my letter so she know I'm okay. I hope she write again, before I go home. Leroy better write too. But I bet he too stupid to give Denise my address so she can write.

"Here we are." Jackie turn up a narrow road in the woods. Look like nobody been here for a long time— flowers and grass growing right in the road. The car bump along over rocks till we come to the top of a hill. Then the road just stop. Jackie pull the brake hard and we get out.

I look around. We in a big open field full of grass and little flowers. It feel like a secret place, it's so sunny and quiet—one bird singing, that's the only noise.

"They sure picked a perfect place for a house, those first settlers," Jackie say.

"I don't see no house." Just grass, bushes, the little flowers—that's all.

"I'll show you." Linda take my hand and pull me through the tall grass. "See—there's the cellar hole where the house was, before it burned down."

"Hey, yeah." I look down at the square hole in the ground, with trees growing up in it and stone walls around the sides. I can't hardly believe this use to be a house.

"Over there was the barn." Jackie point. "And look—lilac bushes, and here's some phlox they planted, probably a hundred years ago, still blooming after all this time." She show me some pink flowers.

"Know how they made the stone walls?" Jimmy ask. "By digging all those rocks out of the ground."

"That used to be open meadow." Jackie point to a little forest of trees. "They had to clear all this land, plant the fields, build a house, and make a life for themselves up here, five miles away from their nearest neighbor . . ." She have a far-off look on her face. "I don't know how they stood those long, lonely winters."

"They should have had snowmobiles," Linda say.

Jackie laugh. "They never dreamed of snowmobiles, back then. Or cars. All they had was a horse and sleigh. No electricity, no telephone, no running water . . . It makes us seem so soft, when you think what those folks went through. Well—" She give us each a basket. "Let's get our raspberries."

We follow her around back of the cellar hole to a field full of tall, bushy plants.

"Look at these berries!" she say. "I never saw so many."

Hey, yeah—I see little red berries all over the plants!

Linda pull one off and give it to me. "Taste."

It look like a little soft red cup. I toss it in my mouth. "Hey, *good.*"

"You said it!" Jimmy pick some for hisself.

"Okay—find a place and start picking," Jackie say. "Look for the dark red ones, B.J. They're the ripest."

I look for a good place and reach in. There a million berries on these bushes. "Ow!" I pull my hand back, with a scratch across it.

"See?" Jimmy say. "That's why we had to wear long pants, because of the stickers." He drop a bunch of berries in his basket.

"We should of wear gloves." I reach out slow for some big ones. "Hey—they all fall off!" I squat down to look for them, but they just tangled-up branches under there. I can't see my berries. They gone.

"The ripe ones always drop off," Jimmy say. "Hold your hand in under them when you pick, like this." He pull off some berries and throw them in his mouth.

Jackie look over. "Come on, Jim. Don't waste time eating. We only have an hour—let's see how many we can pick."

Yeah—I'm gonna fill up my basket fast! I reach for some good ones but they drop off. Let them go, there plenty more. Too bad they so small—it must take about a hundred berries to fill a basket. I go after the next ones slow and careful and drop them in. I got seven so far.

"I found a good place." Linda squat down. "There's lots of good ones down here."

"Here too," Jimmy say, behind me.

Jackie around on the other side. The leaves so thick I can't hardly see her—just her hand, going after the berries. She pick fast.

I look for some good ones. When you go to pick them, half the berries green or pinkish or too-bright red. I eat a pink one, but it so sour I spit it out. All the good berries way in where you can't reach them without getting scratch. These bushes *mean.* Plus, they right out in the sun. I like to take my shirt off, but then I get scratch up worse. My feet sweating in my socks. These dumb branches grab your hat right off your head if you don't look out. I see some big ones down low and go after them. All right—six in a row! Now I got thirteen. Man, this slow. Little bugs start flying around my face.

"Get *off!*" I almost spill my berries, slapping at them.

"You think these bugs are bad," Jimmy say over his shoulder, "you ought to see the black flies in June. They don't just fly around, they *sting* you."

I'm glad I miss them. I already see more bugs in the country than I see in my life—mosquitoes, flies, spiders, moths, big bees, little bees, beetles. Hornets. One night a hornet come in our room and start to dive-bomb our heads! Jimmy catch it in a cup and toss it out the window. He braver than me, man. I hide down under the covers, I'm so scared.

"How you doing, B.J.?" Jackie ask.

"Okay, I guess. Slow." I see some berries right in front of my face and pick them careful. At least the bottom of my basket just about cover. I think this basket too small when Jackie give it to me!

I take off my hat and wipe the sweat off my head.

"Look how many I got." Jimmy show me his basket.

"How you pick all them so fast?" I hold my basket so he can't look in.

"I don't know." He squat down. "Just push the branches around till you see the good ones. Go in under, that's where lots of them are."

I don't like to go under on account of the stickers, but I'm gonna fill up this basket if it kill me. I hold my arm in front of my face and push back some branches and find a good place. Then I start picking. Pull the berries nice and easy, they fall right off in your hand. Stay in one place, move your hand around, that's the way to do it. I reach in under and get a big bunch. Hey, now I'm getting lots of good ones. Me and Jimmy don't even talk, we picking so hard.

Then he stand up. "Look, my basket's full." He take it over to Jackie.

Well, mine almost full. But I'm not stopping till the berries come right to the top. Show Jackie I can pick good. Too bad it so hot out here. My shirt stick right to me, from sweat.

"Mom says we have to go soon." Jimmy come back with a new basket. "This is the only empty one left. When you finish yours we can pick together."

I drop another handful in. That's it—if I put in any more, they roll right out. "I'm finish now." I show Jimmy my basket.

"Set it down somewhere," he say. "Let's try and fill this one before we go."

I set my basket on a flat rock where we won't knock it over. Then me and Jimmy look for a good place to pick.

I find a bush a little way off. "C'mon—I see lots of big ones over here."

He come over and hold the basket where I can reach and we start to pick.

"Too bad we didn't see this place first." Jimmy squat down. "It's the best so far."

"I know it." I reach under a branch. Never mind the prickles, I'm so scratch up now it don't matter. I pick a handful and drop them in.

We going good when Jackie call. "Time to go, guys."

"Mom, wait—we just found a good place!" Jimmy keep picking.

I grab all I can from a high branch. "Hey, Jimmy—look at all the good ones up here."

"*Jim! B.J.!*"

"We're coming." Jimmy pick up our basket.

I toss in my last berries, pull my hat off a branch, and go after him.

"Look how many *we* got." Linda point to the baskets Jackie carrying. I bet Jackie pick most of them, but you can see Linda work hard. Her face and hands all scratch up and her scarf hanging down from one pigtail.

"Let's go," Jackie say. "Walk slow, Jim. Don't spill any berries."

"Hey!" I stop. "My basket!"

Jackie turn around. "Oh, B.J.! Well, run back quick and get it."

"I'll come with you." Linda start to run behind me. "Where'd you put it?"

"On a rock, over there." I point, but I don't see the rock. I can't even see where I was picking. All the bushes look the same. Oh, man. If I lose my good berries . . . !

Linda and me start to hunt on the ground. We look all over, but I still don't see the rock.

Then Linda yell, "I see it!"

I go where she is and there my full basket, right where I set it down.

Yay!

Linda pick it up and start to run.

"Look out!" I yell. "Don't drop it."

"I'm not." She hold it to her chest and keep on running.

"Let *me* carry it." I reach for it, but she duck away.

Jackie honk.

"Come on, Linda." I catch up and grab her arm.

"Oh!" She trip. The basket bounce out of her hand and all the berries spill on the ground.

"Look what you did, dummy!" I start to shake her. Then I look at her face and I let go.

"I didn't mean to drop them, B.J.!" She squat down and scramble around for the berries.

"It's okay." I squat down beside her and start to pick up the berries and drop them back in the basket. "Look—we can get most of them. They just a little dirty, that's all."

Linda wipe her face. "I'm sorry, B.J."

Jackie honk again.

"C'mon." I stand up. "We get most of them, anyway. We get all the good ones." I help her up and give her the basket to carry and we walk back to the car slow and careful.

"What happened?" Jimmy lean out the window.

"Linda find my basket," I say.

Jimmy look at the mess-up berries. "What'd you do, Linda, spill them?"

"Who cares?" I say, quick. "She found them, that's what count." I get in the car after her.

She look at me and smile.

"You know something, B.J.?" Jackie start up the engine. "You're a good kid. We're going to miss you something awful when you go home!"

~~~~~~~~~

"They don't *have* no raspberry in this book!"

I read down the list one more time. Peach, quince, rhubarb, strawberry—

"You know how to spell it?" Jimmy look up. He picking over our berries for leaves and stems and stuff. So far he found two dead bugs and one little live green worm.

"*Yeah,* I know how to spell it." I sound out the word in my head. *"R-A-Z-Z—"*

"Wrong!" he yell. "It's *S-P,* not *Z-Z!*" He think he so smart.

"Yeah, well, I hope you don't ever try to spell jazz *J-A-S-P!*" I go.

He laugh. That's one way he remind me of Leroy—he so easy.

Jackie look over my shoulder. "No wonder you couldn't find it. Look."

I read where she point: *"Blackberry or raspberry, p. 252."*

"Boy—whoever made this index stupid!" I find page 252 and start to read. " 'Mix one-half cup sugar for each cup berries.' "

We wash the berries, measure six cups in a bowl, and pour three cups of sugar on top.

" 'Stir gently, crushing a few of the berries.' " I watch Jimmy stir till the sugar turns pink. " 'Cook over a quick fire. Stir often to keep from sticking. Boil till thick.' "

Jimmy put the pot on the stove and turn the burner on. "I'll stir first."

"I want you both to be careful, now," Jackie tell us. "Stir it slow. When jam starts to boil, it's dangerous."

I know I be careful. There a boy in my school with scars all down his neck and arm from boiling water. I feel sorry when kids stare at him. It's not his fault, how he look.

Jimmy stir for a while. "It's *hot!*" He step back from the pot.

I look in. The juice starting to bubble up. Pink bubbles.

Jimmy face red. "You want a turn?" He give me the spoon. "Don't let it stick."

"I won't." I scrape the spoon across the bottom

and down the sides. This stuff hot! But I'm not gonna complain. I stir a long time before I let myself stop and wipe my face. Then I stir more. "How long we have to do this?" I ask.

"About half an hour," Jackie say. "You can't hurry jam."

Half a hour! I'm ready to pass out *now*. But I keep on stirring.

Jimmy and me trade turns two more times before it start to get thick. "Hey!" I hold up the spoon and blobs of red stuff drop off. "Look—it's almost jam!"

"Want me to take over?" Jimmy reach for the spoon.

"Nah." I'm not quitting now! The stuff starting to, like, sink down in the pot, stick onto the sides and the bottom. It's shiny and thick.

"It's done!" I say.

Jackie give me pot holders and I carry the pot to the sink, where she put the clean jars. I tip the pot over one jar and Jimmy steer the jam in with the spoon. We fill it up.

Jackie take a pot holder and hold the jar up to the window. "Look at that color!" The jam shine like a ruby in the sun.

We fill four more jars. Then Jimmy and me lick the pot. We have to laugh, it taste so good. And we make it ourself!

8

"How does that feel?"

Mr. Hodges, the shoe store man that's Norm friend, pull the shoelace tight, tie a bow, and slap my foot. "Stand up and walk around, B.J. See if they're comfortable."

I step across the rug, wiggling my toes in the shoes. Oh, man, they so cool in the mirror! Leather high-tops, with rawhide laces. Every kid in my school like to have shoes like this.

"They feel good." I walk back to my chair. I hope Norm gonna get me them, but I don't know. They cost $24.95, and Norm and Jackie already buy me a lot of clothes. But Norm say I need shoes like this for camping. We going the day after tomorrow. I can't wait.

"You sure they're big enough?" Norm press the toe of one shoe. "If they rub you anywhere, you want to speak up now. Once we're out in the woods, it's too late."

I guess he *is* gonna buy me them. "No, they fine," I say quick. They stiff around the ankles because I'm not use to high shoes, but they fit good. I bend down to pull up my socks. Look at the tread on these babies! Wait till Leroy sees them. Walk around in shoes like this, everybody think you fresh.

"Okay, then." Norm stand up. "We'll take the two pair, Bill."

Jimmy getting sneakers. He already have shoes like mine. The first time I see them I wish I have a pair. So now I do.

"What do you say, boys?" Mr. Hodges ask. "Want to wear them, or shall I wrap them up?"

"Wear them!" we both say.

I catch a little kid staring at my feet when we go to the counter. I bet he like to be me. Man, am I lucky! I can't believe I got these shoes *plus* all my new clothes: jeans, underwear, a check shirt, and the best of all, a red, like, football sweater with a blue stripe across the front.

Me and Jimmy pick the exact same sweater. When we put them on, Linda say, "Hey, you're twins!" The girl that work there laugh. "Yeah, I can't hardly tell them apart!"

We all laugh, except Linda. At first she don't get it. I think sometimes she forget I'm not her brother, same as Jimmy.

Mr. Hodges put our old shoes in shoe boxes, drop them in plastic bags, and give them to us.

"Well, I guess you're all set for camping," he say to me. "Now you've got yourself a good pair of shoes. Where you planning to take them, Norm, up to the state forest?"

Norm say, "A-yup. We're going to look for a campsite I haven't been to for a long time." He smile. "Not since back in the old days, when you and I were kids." He shake Mr. Hodges hand. "Good to see you, Bill."

"You, too, Norm. And these young fellas." He shake our hands. "Pleased to meet you, B.J."

"Thanks." I shove the door open and we go out.

Norm start down the sidewalk, checking his watch. Jimmy and me have to walk fast to keep up with him. I feel funny in these shoes, like I'm a whole lot taller. I can't stop looking at my feet. I like the way the laces brown on one side, yellow on the other.

"Thanks for the shoes, Norm." I try to match steps with him.

"Yeah, Dad." Jimmy jump up and tap a stop sign. "Thanks for all the stuff you got us."

Norm slow down and smile at us. "Well, we have to keep you kids in style. Hey, Stanley!" He wave at a man in a car. "How ya doing?"

He know a lot of people in this town. I wish I see somebody I know, like Celeste and Sondra, or some other kid from the bus. Jackie say there six or seven Fresh Air Families in Claremont. But so far I don't see no Fresh Air kid.

Jimmy and me duck around a baby carriage and cross the street after Norm. It seem like everybody pick this same day to come and shop. Claremont look small when I first come, but after South Bridgeton it feel like a big city! You think, all these people, some of them be something beside white. But so far all I see is one Chinese-looking lady with a little boy, coming out of Woolworth's. Jimmy say they Vietnamese people that escape from that country in a little boat and come all the way to New Hampshire to live. Jimmy know a boy that go to school with one of the kids. He say when they first come, they can't talk any English. I pity *them,* learning words the way people up here say them!

I guess they use to Fresh Air kids in Claremont, because nobody staring. Some teenage girls outside a store laugh when we go by, but I don't think they laughing at me. Girls always laugh. Like Denise and her friends—just say hello and they break up for no reason.

I see the Grant's sign, right down the block. Now I can't hardly remember the first time I see it, before I know what my family be like. Before I see the house, or the pond. Before I know how to swim. It feel like a long, long time since the day we come here on the bus.

"You have the list, Jim?" Norm stop outside Grant's.

"Yep." Jimmy take it from his pocket. It's a list of

the lumber and stuff we need to make Wiggles new hutch. Norm help me and Jimmy draw up the plans. It so cool how you do it—make a picture on graph paper, measure the lines, and you can see how big the real thing going to be.

Norm know how to build just about anything. Jimmy say he build their whole upstairs bathroom, and the kitchen, too. Somebody else do the plumbing, but that's all. Jimmy too little to help then, but now Norm let him help all the time. The two of them fix the back steps just before I come. Jimmy going to be a carpenter when he grow up. I might be one too—Norm say I be good at it.

"All right, B.J." He hold the door open. "Here it is—the one and only Grant's Hardware."

We go in and walk past the picnic tables and outdoor grills and stripe umbrellas, to a big counter in the middle of the store.

"Hey, Norm!" People look up at us and wave. We go around the counter, past the TV's and window shades and wall tiles and paint cans to a office out in back.

"Jimmy!" A lady jump up from her chair and come and hug him. "Well, B.J.!" she say, like she already know me. "Here you are!"

"This is Ruth Wills, B.J.," Norm say. "Ruth's the one who keeps this whole place running."

Ruth Wills laugh. "Better not say that in front of the boss!"

"Not say what?" A white-hair man with a fat belly come in a different door. He shake hands with Jimmy. "Norm, I believe this boy shoots up a couple inches every time I turn my back!" Then he look at me. "Well, now. This must be—"

"This is my friend B.J.," Jimmy say. "B.J., this is Mr. Grant."

Hey—Mr. Grant, that own the store! I stick out my hand. "Hi."

"Pleased to meet you!" Mr. Grant shake my hand hard. Then he bend down and pretend to whisper in my ear. "The Robertses treating you all right out in South Bridgeton?"

I can tell he just kidding. "They treating me good," I say.

"Fine, fine!" Mr. Grant open a drawer and poke around. "Ruth, have you seen that box of hats we had up here?"

"Try two drawers down." Ruth Wills smile at us. "See what I have to put up with? A boss that can't keep track of his own stock!"

Mr. Grant hold up a green cap. "Give me credit for coming close. There you are, B.J." He put the hat on my head. "That's for you. You know anybody else down there in the Big Apple who might like to wear one of these, do a little advertising for us?"

"Sure," I say quick. "My friend Leroy." Hey—now I have a good present for him!

"Give him this with my compliments." Mr. Grant

hand me a hat. He wink. "And I'd be surprised if a handsome boy like you doesn't have a girlfriend down there in the city who'd like one too." He hold out another one.

Jimmy breaking up behind him, but I don't care. Denise go crazy if I bring her a hat. So why not take it?

I take it. "Thanks, Mr. Grant."

Norm look at his watch. "Time for me to get back to work—I'm late as it is."

"Take some time to show B.J. around first," Mr. Grant say. "Let him see how we do business up in New Hampshire."

"And introduce him to folks," Ruth say. "Everybody wants to meet the New Yorker. You should hear the way Norm's been bragging about you, B.J. I get the feeling he likes having three kids in the family—right, Norm?"

I look at Norm.

"Right," he say.

"And it's nice for you, too, Jimmy," Ruth Wills go on, "having a friend your own age to play with, anytime you want."

"Yeah." Jimmy poke me. "It's good." He almost laughing, but I know he mean it. That's the way he is. Like, if some kid I don't even know come and live in my room, use my stuff, act like my mama *his* mama, *plus* everybody make a fuss over him when we go out, I probably be jealous. Jimmy don't act jealous. Me and him argue and stuff but that's different. Me and Leroy argue all the time. But we friends to the end, just like me and Jimmy.

"How long are you going to be here, B.J.?" Ruth Wills ask.

"Till next Wednesday." That's the first time I say it out loud.

"Oh, my goodness!" she say. "I didn't realize you were going so soon! Well, then, you'll just have to come back another time."

I try not to jump. That's what I think about some nights when I can't go to sleep—coming back here. But I never say it. I don't say nothing now.

Anyway, Norm open the door and push us to it. "We better move on. I have to get these boys some wood, out back."

We say good-bye and go outside. There another whole big part of Grant's in back, call the lumberyard. That's where Norm work. A big tin-roof building, bigger than the store part, with pickups park outside. Inside there a loud saw noise and a wood smell.

Norm take us around and introduce me to all the men he work with. Lenny, Dan, Stub, Eddie—I can't keep track of their names, but they all real friendly. They wink and ask me if Norm treating me right. You can tell they like Norm, the way they kid around with him.

A man behind one of the big saws turn it off, look up, and see us.

"Well, Norm!" he call. "Thought you must have decided to take the day off! Hey, there, Jim—who's your friend?"

"This is B.J.," Jimmy say. "B.J., this is Mr. Hennings."

"Well, now." Mr. Hennings shake my hand. "Pleased to meet you, B.J. How do you like this neck of the woods, after the Big Apple?"

"Good." It seem like everybody up here want to call it that. They must not know that real New Yorkers just call it New York.

"Wes, these boys need some lumber cut to size." Norm lay our plans for Wiggles hutch on the cutting table.

Mr. Hennings study the paper. "Looks all right," he say, after a while. "You fellas work that out yourselves?"

"Dad helped some," Jimmy say.

"Not much." Norm look proud. "It's mostly their design."

"It's all right," Mr. Hennings say again. The way he say it, it's like if a teacher give you a A-plus. "Bring me some two-by-fours, boys, and let's see what we can do. We need ten-footers for this. And half-inch plywood."

Norm show us where to get the wood and Mr. Hennings cut it up for us. He some expert saw-er. He take a piece of plywood, and zap!—he cut it the exact right size.

Then we go across the room to get nails. I never

know there so many kind of nails. We get eight-penny common nails and roofing nails, plus hinges, screws, and a latch for Wiggles front door. Then we get tar-paper and chicken wire. Norm and Mr. Hennings write up a bill, but Norm don't have to pay for it because he work here. We thank Mr. Hennings and carry everything out to the car. We got so much stuff, it look like we making Wiggles a Empire State Building hutch!

"Daddy!" Linda come running across the parking lot. "Look what I got—new sneakers!"

"Hey!" Norm look in her shoe box. "I bet you could win the Boston Marathon with those!"

"They cool, Linda." I stick out my foot. "Look what *I* got." I rub a little dust off one toe. Man, they look so new.

Jackie come up. "How're you doing, guys? Just about finished?" She wipe her face. "I've had it in town—this heat's getting to me. But I have to take Linda down to Cooper's before we go, to look for a school dress."

"Want to go with them," Jimmy ask me, "and check out the models in Woolworth's?"

"Sure." I just as soon sit in the car and rest, but I know he want me to come.

Norm lock up the car and go back to Grant's. Jimmy and me and Jackie and Linda walk down a alley and come out on the main street. There a lot more people in town now. I see two girls pushing a stroller down the street ahead of us. Hey, that look like—yeah, it *is*.

"Celeste!" I yell. *"Sondra!"*

"B.J.!" They look around and stop still in the middle of the sidewalk.

I run up to them. I just about hug Celeste before I stop myself and slap her five.

"How ya doing, girl!" Oh, man, it's cool to see somebody from New York!

"Where you been, B.J.?" Sondra want to know. "We thought you never gonna show up in town!" She wearing a Claremont T-shirt.

"I been around," I say. "Out in South Bridgeton, most of the time. Going swimming and stuff. Only, today we come in to shop." I stick my foot out so she take in my high-tops.

"Hey!" Celeste look down. "Bad! Joyce gonna buy us our shoes tonight, out at the mall." She turn around. *"Joyce! Wesley!* Come here and meet our friend!"

Everybody on the street staring at us, she so loud. But who care? I turn around and look for my family. They kind of hanging back.

"Hey!" I yell. "Come on and meet my friends!"

Linda run up and hide her head in my sleeve.

"This Linda." I poke her. "She real shy—she never talk, right, Linda? This Celeste and Sondra, my friends from the Fresh Air bus. You gonna say hi to them?"

Linda look up and smile. "Hi."

"This my friend Jimmy," I say, when he come up. "The only thing wrong with him, he a Red Sox fan. And this Jackie. This is Sondra and Celeste," I tell her. "From the bus."

Then I look up. *Hey*—a black man and lady coming up the street!

"Joyce! Wesley!" Celeste yell. "Here our friend!"

"This B.J., from the bus," Sondra say to them. "This his family he staying with. This me and Celeste family—Joyce, Wesley, and the baby, Sally. I told you she be cute, right, B.J.?"

Oh, man—I never even notice the baby. She black too! Her face all mess up with cracker crumbs, but she still cute. "Hey, Sally," I say.

Sally bounce in her stroller and laugh.

"She like you!" Celeste say. "Look at her smile!"

The man lean down and shake my hand. "How are you, B.J.? Jimmy?" He shake Jimmy hand. "Hey, there, Linda." He reach for hers.

I'm scared she gonna duck back and act shy, but she don't. She look right up at the man and shake his hand and say "Hi."

Jackie and the lady start talking.

"No, we don't live in Claremont," Jackie say. "But my husband works here, at Grant's. We came to town for the afternoon to do some back-to-school shopping." She kind of laugh. "We put it off till just about the last minute. It's hard to believe they're going back so soon—"

"Oh, I know it!" Joyce look at Sondra and Celeste. "I don't know how we're going to give these girls up, when the time comes. And Sally—I hate to think how the baby's going to miss them, they've been so sweet to her."

"We gonna miss *her.*" Sondra squat down to kiss the baby's head.

"Yeah—" Celeste look sad. "She be all grow up, the next time we come."

"Give me a break!" the man say. "Let me have a couple quiet years, at least, before *this* girl starts turning up the volume, dancing around the house—"

"Wes*ley!*" Celeste sock him. "He crazy, this man," she say, laughing.

"We were just going for ice cream," the lady—Joyce—say to Jackie. "Would you folks like to come with us?"

"I'd love to," Jackie say, "but Linda and I still have to look for a school dress. The boys, though—how about it, kids? We could meet you back at the car in half an hour."

"Sure!" I say.

Jimmy say, "Sure."

I look at him. I think he feeling shy but he know I want him to come.

Jackie look at her watch. "Okay—see you there around four. Don't worry if we're late—it takes a while for the two of us to agree on a dress." She smile at Joyce. "You'll see what I mean when your little girl grows up."

"Oh, I know about *that* already." Joyce laugh. "I'm learning fast, from these girls."

All this time Linda talking to the baby.

"Sally's going to need a friend when Celeste and Sondra go home," Joyce tell her. "So any time you're in Claremont, you come and visit us, okay?"

"Can we, Mommy?" Linda pat the baby head.

"I'd like that," Jackie tell Joyce. "And you come see us in South Bridgeton." Then she wave good-bye to the baby.

The rest of us go around the corner and crowd in a booth at Friendly's, with Sally stroller next to her mother. Man, I'm so glad I see Celeste and Sondra on the street! I feel like laughing just cause we all here.

We order ice cream sodas and the girls start in.

"Hey, B.J., guess what? One time Joyce take us out in a sailboat!"

"Yeah, and one time we go to this place and see five little baby kittens!"

I bust in. "Yeah, well, we got a dog, a rabbit, and five chickens. Right, Jimmy?"

He just nod. I think he feeling out of it cause he the only one not black. But then Wesley ask him about South Bridgeton, and pretty soon Jimmy get loose and he start talking too. It turn out Wesley and Joyce schoolteachers. You can tell they the good kind. Wesley remind me of my daddy, the way he laugh from way down deep in his stomach.

I slurp up my ice cream soda from the bottom of my glass and watch Sondra play peekaboo with the baby. This just about my best time since I come up here. Only, I can't stop thinking about my daddy. I bet he like to sit here and laugh with my friends. I wish he have a good job like Wesley, so he feel like he okay. Mama always telling him, "Be somebody." But he already somebody. He my daddy.

Guess what? It seem like he hear what I'm thinking, because when we go back to South Bridgeton there a letter waiting for me!

> Dear Son,
> Your Mama say you in the country, with some nice folks. I hope you having a good time. Well, I got good news. A factory just open up in the Bronx and your Daddy get a job on the night shift. How about that? So now things looking up!
> I hope to see you soon, son, when you come home. You get set to tell me all about the country.
>
> > Your loving Daddy,
> > Baxter Johnson.
>
> P.S. Here five dollars. You buy your friends a soda or ice cream.

Oh, man! "Guess what?" I'm so glad to tell Jackie. "My daddy get a job!"

"Hey, he fly away!"
I chase across the grass after the lightning bug.

But just when I almost catch him, he zoom off again.

"Look how many I got!" Linda hold up her jar. A whole lot of bugs blinking on and off inside it. "I'm taking them in to show Daddy." She run to the house. The screen door slam.

"I'm letting mine go." Jimmy flop down on the grass and take the lid off his jar.

"Wait!" I grab his hand but it too late. The bugs fly out, turning on and off like little flashlights.

"What you do that for?" I sit down next to him.

"They like to be free." Jimmy lay back with his hands behind his head.

I lay back too. We watch the bugs fly up and up to the sky. It's so quiet we can hear Linda and Norm talking in the kitchen. Music on TV down the street. A mosquito, buzzing around our heads. My own heart, thumping slow.

The whole big sky hanging over us. I never see sky so dark, or stars so bright.

"*Look* at all them stars." I pull up a grass blade and bite on it. "I bet there millions of them up there." The sky like a giant movie screen, spread over the whole world. You could get dizzy, looking up through space all the way to the stars.

"There's *billions*," Jimmy say. "And you know what? All those ones we can see are just in our

Earth's galaxy. Out beyond them, there's a billion *more* galaxies, going on and on to infinity."

"I know." I try to sound cool, but my heart just about stop beating, thinking about it. I spread out my arms on the grass. I feel like I'm hanging on to my place on this one little star we riding on. Earth.

Then Norm come out and call, "Time for bed, guys," and Jimmy and me get up and walk back to the house, under all the bright stars.

9

"Foo!" I spit out a bug that fly right in my mouth. "I hate these dumb bugs!"

I feel like I'm talking to Jimmy backpack, cause he never turn around. The way he swing up the trail, like he climbing a escalator, his pack must not bother him. Mine keep poking me in the back. I like to stop and fix it, but I can't take the time because I'm trying to keep up. I don't know how long we got to go before we get there. We already hike at least a hour. My feet killing me, in my new shoes. They good shoes, but they heavy.

Norm way up ahead somewhere, looking for the trail to the campsite. We following the trail with blue blazes. Blazes—that's the marks somebody before us paint on the trees to show where the trail go.

Norm say lots of people been in these woods before us—Indians, loggers, hunters, even some farmers that clear all this land and build houses and stone walls and wagon roads on it before they go away and the trees grow up again.

But now we the only ones around, maybe for miles. I can't get use to the idea that all this, like, nature always be here, even if nobody here to see. We just go past a giant tree on the ground that must of make a horrible crash going down, except probably no person even hear it. That's *weird.*

But it's not scary in the woods like I think before we come. It's more like walking in a big sunny green room. We can't get lost because Norm bring his compass and a trail map, and it's easy to follow the blazes. Anyway, I know what to do if I did get lost—look for a brook and walk the way the water going. Norm say sooner or later every brook run down to a river. Follow the river, you gonna come to people. It could take a long time, though. I wouldn't like to sleep alone out here, in the woods after dark.

"Hey, B.J.!—look up here!"

Jimmy stop at the top of the path. I don't know how he get ahead of me so fast.

"I'm coming." I shove my backpack straight and try to walk faster. Hiking uphill make you get out of breath. At least, when you play hoop, the court *flat.* I grab on to some little tree trunks and heave myself up till I get to where Jimmy at.

"See?" He wave his arm around. "It's a planted forest."

"Hey, yeah!" There rows and rows of trees around us, all the same size, like corn plants in a garden. Big tall trees that shut the sun out so it cool and dark underneath. The ground like a soft brown carpet.

"Man, these trees big." I rest my pack against a trunk and look up.

"Yeah," Jimmy say. "White pines. Somebody must have planted them about a hundred years ago."

"How you know that?"

"Because that's how long it takes for white pines to get this big."

"I mean, how you know they white pines?"

"You just do." Jimmy shrug. "From how the needles look, and the bark, and the way the low branches die back when the tops grow up."

It's amazing, all the stuff Jimmy know. Him and Norm, both. They always looking around, seeing things. Just since we come in the woods, Norm show me a tree trunk with woodpecker holes punch around it in rows, like a machine drill them. Jimmy show me a little stripe chipmunk scooting across the path with his tail in the air, and a toad the exact same color as a rock. Norm know all the different mushrooms. We see a orange one that, if you eat one little tiny bite of it, you dead. I don't even go *near* it.

It's cool to know stuff like that. You feel more, like, *part* of nature if you know about it. Just like you a real New Yorker when you know the trains and the subway stops.

"Hey, down there!" Norm call.

"We're coming!" Jimmy call back.

We pull up our packs and start to walk through the trees. The ground in here feel good on my feet, it so soft and spongy. I wouldn't mind hiking all day in here, except for my pack. My pack weigh fourteen pounds—I know, cause we put them on the bathroom scale to see. I got half our food in it, my long-sleeve shirt, sweater, extra socks, the first-aid kit, and a canteen. Plus my sleeping bag strap to the outside. At least Norm take the tents. That's why his pack weigh twenty-seven pounds. Poor him.

Jimmy stop in front of me. "Want some trail mix?"

"Sure." I untie the cord of his pack pocket and take out the bag of raisins, nuts, and sunflower seed we fix this morning.

I dump out half in his hand and we go on walking, throwing pieces in our mouths. Trail mix suppose to give you energy. It's good. Up here, lots of things that's good for you taste good, too, like fresh-pick vegetables and whole wheat bread, and this stuff. I hold up the bag and shake out the last crumbs in my mouth. Then I crumple the bag and toss it.

"Hey!" Jimmy stop and pick it up. "Don't throw trash down in the woods."

"Why you on my case? Who gonna see it, way out here?"

"Anybody that comes along." He stuff the bag in

his pocket and go on. "That could be a lot of people, in a year," he say over his shoulder.

"A year!" I laugh. "You think that bag gonna lay there for a whole year? It probably blow off in five minutes, if you don't pick it up."

"So? Wherever it blew to, it would still *be* there." He duck under a low branch. "Plastic lasts forever. Besides, if everybody threw trash on the trail, the whole woods would turn into a dump."

He sound like my teacher! *If everybody just threw down one little tiny piece of paper, this whole school would look like a trash pile.* Which my school look like, anyway. It's different out here, with all this space. But why argue? I don't want to mess up the woods, even if Jimmy think I do.

"Hey, guys!" Norm call again.

Now we out of the pine forest, I can see where he calling from—way on top of the hill in front of us. I can make out his blue shirt. Oh, boy. Look like it's a long way up to where he at.

We call and wave and start up the path. I let Jimmy go first. He always want to go fast. I would go fast, too, except this pack so heavy and my shoes keep rubbing my feet. It feel like I'm getting a blister on one heel.

We go up a little way and then the path get *steep.* There no good place to put your feet. I try to step in the same place as Jimmy, but I can't see good from behind him. I'm practically hauling myself up by my hands now, holding on to rocks and tree roots.

"Hey!" I trip, catch hold of a branch, and the branch snap right off! I start to slide back down the path.

Jimmy turn around. "You okay?"

"Yeah." I grab another branch and pull myself up again. "I just trip, that's all."

I fix my pack one more time, brace my foot on a tree trunk, and take a big step up. I hope Jimmy can't hear how loud I'm breathing. This path so steep you could pass out just going up it. I wouldn't *mind* passing out for about five minutes—I could use the rest.

But I got to keep going. Step, haul myself up, step, haul up—so much sweat running down my face I can't hardly see. I feel my blister puff up inside my one shoe. Soon as we get there, I'm gonna take off my shoes and socks. Give my feet some *air.*

Jimmy up near Norm. I hear him ask, "You find the path, Dad?"

"Yeah," Norm say. "It's right here. The campsite should be close."

Yay—we getting there! If I can just make this last part . . . But it's the steepest of all.

"How're you doing, B.J.?" Norm call down.

I open my mouth—and step on a loose rock.

"Aaagh!" I slip and slide down the path on my stomach. Rocks scraping my front. Help! I grab for a branch. It break. I'm sliding faster—*help!* I hit a tree, hang on to it, and stop.

Oh, man! I lay there shaking. My heart pounding like a hammer in my chest.

"You all right?" Norm yell. "Need some help?"

"No!" I take a deep breath, hang on to the tree, and pull myself up slow. I hurt all over but it look like nothing break. My pack still on me. I wipe my face and start to crawl back up on my hands and knees. I'm not gonna stop till I get to the top. Show them I can do it. Man, this a long way up. I feel like a baby, crawling on the ground, but I got to make it any way I can. Just let me go slow and easy, brace myself so I don't slip. I'm getting closer all the time. Closer. There some big roots up here to hold on to. I grab one and pull myself up. Then another one.

"Looking good, B.J."

Norm standing right over my head. I'm almost there!

He lean over and hold out his hand—

I grab it, step, and Norm heave me up.

"All right!" Jimmy slap me on the pack.

I made it! I stand there and catch my breath. Then I lift up my shirt. Oh, boy, scratches all over my chest.

"Hey—I bet that hurts." Jimmy look at the scratches.

"Some." I'm not gonna complain, if it kill me.

Norm get out the first-aid kit and open up a tube. "This'll stop the stinging. Keep it clean too." He spread some cool stuff on my front.

"That last part was rough," he say. "You did good, B.J."

I *feel* good. Like I come through some kind of test.

"Look at the view from up here!" Jimmy say. I go where he standing and look out through the trees. Hey, yeah—rows and rows of blue mountains, rolling way off to the sky. Beautiful!

"See down there, that little clearing?" Jimmy point. "There's our car."

"I see it!" I shoo a bug away and wipe the sweat off my face. "We come a long way up, man."

"Yeah."

It feel like we explorers. Like, two brothers that just discover this mountain, and Norm could be like a mountain man that guide us.

"Ready to go?" he ask. "There's our trail, where that yellow blaze is. If I remember right, the campsite's just a little way on."

I hope he remember right.

We heave up our packs and start off—Norm, then me, then Jimmy. The path go along the mountaintop, flat and easy. I bet there nobody high as us for miles. In New York, you have to go on top of the World Trade Center to get this high up. Cram in a elevator with people just waiting to buy souvenirs. I don't need no souvenir from here—I just want to remember how it look, way, way off to the blue mountains. I'm remembering that for my whole life. Wait for a train in some dirty subway station, all I have to do is close my eyes and see the mountains in my mind.

Jimmy pull a piece of bark from a tree. "That's birch bark. The Indians made canoes from it."

"Hey, birch bark canoes—we had that in school!" I like to show my teacher. "Can I keep it?"

"Oh, sure," he say. "Take more, if you want. It just falls off the trees, anyway."

So I pull off some big loose strips, and he help me roll them up and stuff them in my backpack.

"There's our turn." Norm point to a tree with two blazes on it. He already tell us two blazes mean a turn.

We start down a path through some bushes, walk a little way, and come out in a field of soft grass, with birch trees all around, like a little secret meadow in the woods.

"This is it." Norm shake off his pack. "How do you like it?"

"Good!" we both say.

"Looks like we're the first ones to come here this summer." Norm take the tent bags out of his pack.

I flap up my shirt to give my chest some air. If I know all we have to do to get here, I might not want to go camping. Only now I'm so glad we come.

"Let's get moving." Norm toss one tent bag over to me and Jimmy. "Pitch our tents, find firewood—we want to get set up before dark."

Jimmy open the bag. "It's a long time till dark."

"You wait—it'll come fast, once the sun goes down behind that mountain." Norm walk around, checking out the ground. "How about you guys pitching your tent here, and I set mine up over there?"

"Sure, here looks good." Jimmy dump out the tent pieces on the grass and pick up two short poles. "You can start putting these together, B.J. See how they go?" He shove one inside the other.

"Yeah." Only I can't make mine go together. What *is* this? Oh, yeah, I see—you got to put the thin end in the thick one. I do all the short poles and Jimmy push stakes in the ground for the tent corners. Then we push the long poles together. It's cool how all the pieces fit—poles, stakes, and then the tent cloth on top, fasten to the stakes with metal rings. Hey, now it's a real tent!

We finish before Norm, so we help him fix his tent. The field look so good with both tents up. Like a picture of people camping out. And we the ones that doing it!

"C'mon." I get my pack. "Let's fix up our sleeping bags."

"Lay this down first." Norm give me a piece of plastic. "Keep the damp out."

Me and Jimmy shove the plastic in the tent, pull it straight, and roll out our sleeping bags on top. We have to crawl inside the tent to pull them straight. Oh, man, it's so cool in there—like a little house with a front door flap. Me and Jimmy lay back on our sleeping bags and look out through the flap at the sunny grass.

"Man, this the life." I swat at a mosquito over my head. "Except for the bugs. I wonder if that one mosquito follow us up here, or if he already here, waiting."

"That's what I always wonder," Jimmy say. "Like, how do mosquitoes know somebody's coming for supper?" He laugh. "Maybe they have spies down at the parking lot."

"Yeah! Maybe—"

Norm lift up the flap. "All set?"

"Yeah." I like to just lay here in the tent and relax. Take my shoes off.

But he say "Come on out, then. We have to look for firewood and fill our canteens at the brook."

We crawl out of the tent, get our canteens, and follow Norm down a narrow path through the birch trees.

He stop in front of me and bend down. "Deer sign."

I look around. "I don't see no sign."

Jimmy laugh. "There." He point with his foot. "See? That's deer shit."

I stare at the pile of little balls. They almost the same size as Wiggles, only more light color. "You think we might see a deer?" I ask. I like to see one live. There a picture of a deer in my school library. If I see a real one, I can tell the librarian. Only I'm not telling her about no sign.

"We might see one," Norm say. "That's fresh sign.

The deer probably come down this way to the brook. Look, there's a track."

"Hey, yeah!" I bend down and look at the pointy hoof marks. "You ever see a deer?" I ask Jimmy.

"Sure, lots of times, in the woods. Plus, all the ones Dad shot and brought home."

"You shoot *deer?*" I look at Norm. How could he do that?

He look at me. "I've gone deer hunting just about all my life," he say slow. "I guess that sort of surprises you, doesn't it?"

I nod my head. I'm staring down at the track that a real, live deer just make, that a hunter—Norm!—could come along and kill. It don't just surprise me, it make me *mad*.

Norm lay his hand on my shoulder. "I know it's hard for you to understand. But up here, in the country—"

I shake off his hand and walk on by myself. I got to think. Norm not a bad man—he the best man I ever know except my own Daddy. I don't see how he could kill a deer, in cold blood.

Jimmy come after me. "Shooting's only part of it, B.J. Hunting's, like, a *sport*. You might have to track the deer for miles, before you even see one. And then, if it sees you, it can still get away . . ."

I just look at him.

"Everybody hunts, in the country." He start to talk faster, like he trying to convince hisself. "And it's not a waste, because of the meat. Lots of people, that's what they eat all winter, deer meat."

He wait for me to answer. But I don't. I can't.

"Well, where do you think hamburger comes from?" he say. "You know what hamburger is? Dead cow, that's all. Dead cow that *some*body had to kill."

"Jim." Norm right behind us. "That's enough." I can feel him looking at the back of my head. "It's hard to explain," he say, like he thinking out loud, "the hold hunting gets on you, if you've done it all your life. Get up at dawn on a cold November morning, watch the mist burn off and the hills light up in the sun . . ."

He practically beside me, now, but I don't look at him.

"I'm not trying to excuse it, B.J. But it's a fact that there's too many deer for these woods to support. Without a hunting season to thin out the herd, they could all die of starvation. And Jim's right, there's a lot of families up here need the meat."

I nod. I still feel sorry for the deer. For all dead animals. I like to say I never eat hamburger again. I know I will, but I know I'm never gonna shoot a deer, in my whole life.

"There's the brook." Jimmy cut across a muddy place.

I come after him, trying not to get my shoes wet. The brook splashing over the rocks in little waterfalls.

Leafs and sticks floating on top of it, little shiny stones on the bottom.

Jimmy kneel down on the bank to drink.

I take off my shoes and socks and stick my hot feet in the water. Hoo, man—cold as ice! I wiggle my toes. They so free! I got a blister on my one heel, but I'm not telling Norm. I can get a Band-Aid from the first-aid kit, later on.

Jimmy and me slosh around in the water till we cool off. Norm take off his hat and duck his head right in. Then we drink, fill up our canteens, and start back to the campsite.

"I don't know about you," Norm say, "but I'm getting hungry."

"Yeah." I can't keep from talking to him. It's not his fault he raise up to go hunting, like all country people. But I still hate it.

Norm pick up a piece of wood from the side of the path. "Keep an eye out for firewood—small pieces like this, that's what burns best."

There a lot of wood just laying on the ground, once you start to look. I pick up a good piece. "Come out here, you get a whole woodpile, free."

"Wait a minute." Norm laugh. "That's *if* you take a day off to come and find it, maybe two, three days, cut it up, haul it out to a road, load it on a truck, drive it home—and then you still have to cut it in stove lengths. That's not the same as free." He pick up a birch log. "The way we get wood, I order a couple cords delivered. Have them dump it out back of the barn and saw it up myself. Then me and my helper"—he lay his hand on Jimmy shoulder—"stack it up in a woodpile, and we're set for winter."

Jimmy make a face. "Yeah, you know how much Dad paid me, for two days' work?"

We hear a funny, like, cough, behind us.

Norm stop still, so sudden that I bump into him. "Look, B.J.!" He grab hold of me. "See there?"

I just see trees. Then something move. Oh, hey—I see it—a *deer*, standing like a statue under the branches.

Stay still, I tell it, in my head. *Let me just look at you!*

The deer don't move. I see his big ears, soft brown body, white tail . . . I hold my breath. For just a minute, it feel like the deer and us *together*, looking at each other. Then the deer flick an ear, turn, hang there a second—and leap up, like a dancer, and fade off through the trees.

"Did you see it?" Jimmy whisper.

"Yeah." I let my breath out. I can't hardly believe what I see, it happen so fast.

"All the times I've come on a deer in the woods, it still takes my breath away." Norm touch my shoulder. "I'm glad you got to see one, son."

"Yeah." My heart still pounding from the beauty of it. I hope the deer have a safe place to hide, where

no hunter ever find it. I think Norm and Jimmy hope
the same thing.

We stand there a minute, staring at where the deer
go. Then we walk back to the camp.

Norm show us how to make a safe campfire. Look
for bare dirt, away from any trees. Lay a circle of
stones around it. Lean some little sticks up like a
tepee, stick dry bark under them, light it with a
match. Let the fire catch good, then lay on the big
pieces, one at a time.

We unpack all the food we bring in our packs: hot
dogs, rolls, can spaghetti, can peas, carrot sticks,
apples, and peanut butter cookies Jackie make us last
night, plus marshmallows to cook on the fire. Everything we need to cook and eat with fit in one cooking
kit—pots, pot lids that make plates, a pot handle,
cups, and each person knife, fork, and spoon that
snap together in a set.

We roll a big log up to the fire. When the food hot
we fill our plates, sit on the ground, and lean against
the log to eat. We don't even talk—just relax, eat,
and watch the sun go down through the trees. Every
single bite of food delicious, even the burn part of the
hot dog rolls. Carry food on your back all the way up
a mountain, it bound to taste good when you get
there and sit down and eat it.

When we finish our supper and the fire burn down,
Jimmy and me cook marshmallows on sticks. I eat

marshmallows before at school parties, but they something else when you cook them. We squat down and hold our sticks in the coals till our faces feel like they burning up. It take a long time to cook marsh-mallows right—crusty brown on the outside, runny on the inside. But it's worth it. Eat a puff-up marsh-mallow right off the stick, that's *good*. Me and Jimmy cook extras for Norm. He stretch out on the ground with his back against the log and drink his coffee, watching us make them.

"B.J., that one looks ready to me," he say. "I can't wait much longer."

"Just one more second!" I hold it up to look. "This my best one so far—"

Aaaowoooooooo!

I drop my stick in the dirt. "What was *that!*"

Jimmy laugh. "Just an old owl. Scary, huh?"

"Yeah!" I pick up the marshmallow, pull off the outside, and give what left to Norm. That some crazy call—halfway between a dog and a bird. I'm ready for it the next time, but I still jump when I hear it. I go sit down by Norm. I can't help it, I'm scared. We the only human beings in these whole woods. And the sky turning dark.

"How about a story?" Norm poke a stick in the fire so it glow up bright. Then he start telling about olden times, back when he was a kid. Guess what, one time he spill a whole plate of bake beans on the ground when a owl hoot at him from a tree. Then he throw

his hot dog up at the owl, and it come right back
down on his head, with ketchup on it!

Pretty soon Norm have us laughing so hard I forget
to be scared. I'm surprise—back home, he don't talk
that much. But the way he tell stories, he good as Bill
Cosby! Every time he stop, Jimmy get him going
again: "Tell how you lost the canoe paddles in the
lake!" "Tell about your winter underwear." Norm
must have a hundred stories to tell. I like to hear all of
them.

When we so full we can't eat another marshmallow, we lean against the log and watch the sky turn
orange and purple and then dark-blue.

"I see the first star!" Jimmy point. "Star light, star
bright—"

"First star I see tonight," I say it with him.

"Wish I may, wish I might, have the wish I wish tonight!" we finish together.

"What'd you wish for?" he ask me.

"I'm not telling. That spoil it."

"Okay, then I'm not telling, either."

"Don't, I don't care." Anyway, wishes suppose to
be private.

"How about it—time to hit the sack?" Norm stand
up and stretch. Back home, Jimmy and me probably
say it too early for bed, but up here we don't. I'm
tired, plus, I can't wait to go in the tent.

But we have to clean up first. We help Norm put
out the fire good. We wash our dishes with the end of

Norm's coffee water. Then we take our canteens and go off under the trees and rinse our mouths and pee. I stand under a big white pine and listen to the night noises. I wonder if the deer still out there. I hope he safe.

The stars come out more when we get undress. Every single little star sparkling. I shiver. It's cold up here!

"C'mon!" Jimmy crawl under the tent flap. "Get in where it's warm."

I crawl inside after him. Our flashlight light up the whole tent. We take off our shoes and set them near the flap so we can find them in the morning. Then we climb in our sleeping bags and zip them up. Oh, hey. We camping out!

"You guys all set?" Norm squat down by the tent flap. "I'll be right here in my tent. If you need me, just call. Okay, B.J.?"

"Yeah." I'm glad his tent close to ours.

"Okay, Jim?"

"Yeah," Jimmy say. "Good night, Dad."

"Good night, Norm," I go.

"Good night, boys. Sleep well." He stand up. I hear him walk over to his tent and get in. I bet he like somebody there to sleep beside of.

I slide down in my sleeping bag and turn over. But I can't lie on my stomach because my scratches hurt, so I have to turn over again.

"Hey!" Jimmy say. I guess I kick him by mistake.

"Sorry." Boy, this ground hard. I didn't expect it to feel so bumpy. It look flat when we put the tent up. Now I can't get comfortable any way I turn around. I unzip my bag and push the top part down. I'm hot. A mosquito buzz around my neck. My blister start to hurt. I forget to put on a Band-Aid. Now it's too late.

"I bet I'm never gonna go to sleep." I roll over on my side and shove Jimmy. See if he awake.

He say, "Yeah," but two seconds later, he snoring. He don't lay still, though. He bounce around in his bag. Every time he move, he kick me. I try to push him off, but he flop right back again.

I start thinking about my good bed back at the house. Nice cool sheets, pillow, soft mattress—I like to climb in there right now. Instead of lay here on the hard ground, with a mosquito buzzing in my ear, and Jimmy kicking me every two seconds. Snoring. I bet Norm snoring too.

Crack!

What was that? I hold my breath and listen. Something out there, near the tent! Something *live*—I hear it walking around. I sit up in the dark. I can't see out, but I hear the noise come closer. It sound like some big animal. Oh, no! What if it—the word jump in my head—a *bear!*

Jimmy snore.

I kick him to shut him up. I got to call Norm. Except then the bear hear me.

Whatever out there, he right by the campfire. I

hear him knocking our pans around. Norm better wake up and do something! Only what if the bear go after *him?*

I crawl to the door and find the flashlight. I know what I got to do—I got to go out there. Grab me a piece of wood and chase that bear off. I got to save us all!

I raise the tent flap slow, crawl out on the ground, and stand up with the flashlight in my hand. Then I make a run for the campfire and grab a log.

"AAAGH! Get away! Go!" I snap the flashlight on.

"Hey!" A fat little animal shoving a tin plate around on the dirt. He have a long nose, little bright eyes, a thick tail, and, like, *needles* sticking out all over his body.

"What's going on?" Norm stumble out of his tent in his underwear. He look at the animal and he look at me. Then he laugh.

"B.J.—it's just a porcupine!" He pick up a stone and throw it down in front of the animal. "Go on—get out of here! Shoo!"

The porcupine back off the plate and waddle off across the grass, heading for the trees. He fat, but he moving fast. I bet he scared!

Norm come over to me. "B.J., you okay?"

"Yeah." I'm shaking. "I think I hear a bear!" I feel stupid.

Norm don't laugh at me. "There's no bears around here, but you were brave to get up and check." He lay his hand on my shoulder. "Now—think you can go back to sleep?"

"Yeah." I can't go *back* to sleep, but now I'm going.

Norm give a little push. "Good night, son."

"Night." I lift up the tent flap, crawl inside, and climb back in my sleeping bag. Oh, boy. The ground still hard, but it feel *good*.

Jimmy snoring. I stretch out my legs slow, so I don't kick him. I bet *he* laugh at me in the morning. Let him laugh, I don't care. Anyway, now Norm know I'm brave.

"Hello, folks!" Jackie come up to our table with her order pad. "Here's the customers I've been waiting for—three good-looking kids, and"—she give Norm a little shove with her hip—"a handsome man!"

Norm duck and smile. My daddy use to smile like that when Mama sweet-talk him.

I like Mama to see this restaurant. Red leather booths, tables with white cloths, lamps, red check curtains on the windows. Good-smelling food. Mama won't go in no restaurant that smell like old cooking grease. She want to eat in style if she eat out.

I catch some people smiling at us when Jackie

take our orders. I bet they can tell we her family.
Everybody that work here act like we special.
And it seem like they all know about me. When
we come in, the lady that take us to our table
bend down and whisper, "I bet your ears have
been burning, the way Jackie boasts about you!"
And the man that bring our water say he want to
meet the New Yorker. "That's my ambition," he
say, "to live in New York City."

We go to the salad bar before Jackie bring our
dinners. You can take all you want. Me and
Jimmy fill our plates so full our pickle beets run
in the applesauce. Norm don't say nothing, but
he make Linda stop taking cherry tomatoes after
about ten.

We go eat our salad, plus hot biscuits with
honey, and then Jackie bring our dinners—spaghetti for Linda, hamburgers and mash potatoes
for me and Jimmy, a ham steak for Norm. We
dig in and eat till we empty our plates. This good
food!

Then a fat man in a yellow shirt come out of
the kitchen and head for our table. "Well, how
are all you folks?" he say. "Glad to have you
here. Going to introduce me to this young fella?"
It turn out he Sandy, that own the whole Sandy's
Diner. "Dessert on the house," he say. That mean
free!

We all choose raspberry pie with ice cream.

Jackie bring it out. Now I know Norm right—
raspberry the best kind of pie. I eat my whole big
piece, even the bare crust.

Then Jackie take me back to see the kitchen.
Go through the swing door, you in a whole different place, like backstage at a play. The restaurant
dark and quiet, but the kitchen bright and noisy
and hot. Everybody rushing around yelling—
cooks slapping food on plates, waitresses grabbing
up dishes. You think they never get it together
and take everybody their right dinner, the way
they do.

Jackie introduce me to two cooks, the dishwasher, a busboy, and three waitresses. Then
Sandy give me a bag of doughnuts for our breakfast, and Jackie and me go out the back door.
She tell us good night at the car because she staying on to work.

"How about some music?" Norm turn on the
radio and we sing along, the whole way home.
Jimmy and me roll around on the back seat and
groan, we so full. But I don't care how stuff I
am—this still my best time I ever eat in a restaurant, in my whole life.

10

"Hold *still*, Lucky!"

He standing on my lap with his head out the car window, yipping. Slobbering with joy, cause he coming with us. We park outside the post office waiting for Jackie. I never see Lucky act so excited.

"You're glad you're going with us, aren't you, Lucky?" Linda pat his behind.

"Wait till he sees where we're going." Jimmy turn around from the front seat. "He's gonna go crazy when we get to the pond."

"I hope he go in. I want to see him swim." I shove Lucky tail out of my face.

"He will," Jimmy say. "Just throw a stick in the water, he'll run after it."

"Can he always find it?" I ask.

Jimmy laugh. "No, half the time he loses it. Then he just brings you back a stone or something. He's not a real retriever."

Lucky see a dog go by and just about throw hisself out the window, barking.

"C'mon, Lucky." I haul him back in.

Linda shove his rear end down. "Sit! Show how good you behave in the car, or Mommy's gonna take you back home."

But Lucky wriggle out from under her hand, spring for the front seat, and dive over on top of Jimmy.

"Hey!" Jimmy grab him. "The only way to make this dog sit, is sit *on* him," he say. "You guys have to take care of him at the pond—you're the ones that wanted to bring him."

"We will." I reach over and scratch Lucky neck the way he like me to. I'm glad Jackie let us bring him. I think she let us because this my last time at the pond. She don't want me to feel bad if I can't make it to the raft. I hope I can. I want to see what it's like to be out there just one time, before I go.

Jackie come out of the post office with the mail. "Another one for you, B.J.!"

"Thanks!" I already get two letters yesterday! One from Mama, the other from Leroy. Maybe this be from—

"Who's it from?" Linda try to see.

"Nobody." I check out the address. Hey, yeah, it *is* from Denise!

"I bet it's from his girlfriend." Jimmy look around.

"So?" I open the envelope slow and cool and take my letter out.

Linda grab the envelope from my lap. "Here's who it's from—"*D-E*—"

"Denise!" Jimmy yell. "I knew it! *Now* B.J.'s happy, because his girlfriend wrote him a letter!"

"You just jealous," I say fast, "cause no girl dumb enough to waste a stamp on you."

"Dear B.J." Jimmy put on a foolish voice. "Please come home soon, because my heart is breaking!"

"Shut up!" I reach over the seat to poke him.

"Come on, kids," Jackie say. But I catch her smiling in the mirror. "I think it's nice that your girlfriend wrote to you," she say.

Man! They act like Denise letter a major news event! Even Lucky—he scrabble back over the seat, stick his face in my letter, and mess it all up with his drool.

"Move!" I push him away so I can read.

Dear B.J.
　　I bet you surprise to get a letter from me!

I'm not all *that* surprise. I *think* Denise like me. Except with girls you never sure.

　　Well, don't get excited. I'm only writing cause Jackie Romero make me write. See, Jackie come over my house, and I go, it's boring, nothing to do, and she go, *I* know what to do, write a letter to B.J. So I go, Why should I write to that boy if he never write to me? Then Jackie go, Ha, ha, I bet you scared to write because B.J. think you after him. I say, Girl, I don't care what he think, only he better not think I'm scared, cause I'm not. And here my letter to prove it.

Boy! I have to laugh. Denise *crazy.*

Jackie and me gonna go see if Leroy have the address where you at in the country. So if you get this letter, you know he give it to us.

At least old Leroy not too dumb to know he suppose to.

I bet it's nice up there in the country. It's *boring* around here. I be glad when summer over. At least school something to do.

Well, stay cool, don't be a fool, and I see you in school.

From,
Denise Simpson.

P.S. You better *not* think I'm after you!!!

I read the whole letter two times. Now I *know* Denise like me. So what if she don't put "Love, Denise"? I rather have a crazy girlfriend than some girl just thinking about love all the time.

"What did she say?" Jimmy want to know. "Did she say, 'My honey, I love you so much?' "

"She say, 'Tell your stupid friend to shut his mouth!' " I fold up my letter and stuff it in my pocket. I'm keeping all my letters I get in the country so I can read them again if I want.

Jackie turn down the pond road and Lucky lean out the window.

"I think he knows where we are," Linda say.

"He ought to," Jackie say. "He's spent a lot of summer days out here. Right, Lucky? Know where we are?" She pull up the brake. "At least there's only two other cars," she say. "So he won't bother too many people."

Lucky burst out soon as she open the door. He start to run around in circles, sniffing the ground.

"Come on, Lucky." Linda get out. "Let's go see the water."

She take off down the path with Lucky after her. You can tell Lucky old, the way he run stiff-legged. But he bark like he a little happy puppy.

Jackie watch him go. "Poor thing, he's getting stiff. I'm glad we brought him, though. Let him see the pond again, he loves it so much."

"Come on, B.J." Jimmy say.

"Wait a second, Jim." Jackie take my arm. "I need to say something to B.J. first." She pull me over by a tree.

I wait. I can tell she want to say something heavy.

"I'm going to write your mom a note, before you go home," she start. "And one thing I'm going to tell her is, I'm proud of how you learned to swim. The way you kept at it every day and didn't give up.

"Now, listen." She look me in the eye. "I know how bad you want to go out to the raft today. And I think you're just about ready to do it. But I want you to re-member—swimming to the raft, or not swimming to the raft, isn't what counts. What counts is that you *can* swim. Right?"

When Jackie eyeball you like that, you got to say something.

"Yeah," I say.

"I know your mother's going to be real proud of you." Jackie give me a little shake. "All right, then, Jim," she call. "You and B.J. bring the things—I'm going on to see how Linda's doing with Lucky."

Jimmy reach in the car and pull out our stuff. "What did Mom want?" he ask.

"Nothing." I take a towel and head down the path. "Just, it's good I can swim."

"Well, it is," Jimmy say quick. "So what if you don't go out to the raft? It's just a place to sit, that's all. You can sit anywhere."

I don't say nothing back. I bet *he* want to go to the raft when he learning to swim. Everybody want to go there. It's the best place at the pond.

"If you want to try and swim out there, I'll swim with you." He look at me kind of careful.

"I let you know." I don't want him hanging around me. When I'm ready, I can tell Jackie to watch me and go out by myself. I rather go by myself.

I look at the ferns alongside the path. I like to always remember going down this path. How you start off in shade, on the cool dirt, and come out on burning-hot sand. And see the water sparkling in the sun. I bet this the prettiest pond in New Hampshire.

I see Linda and Lucky down by the water edge. Lucky jumping around and yipping with joy.

"Uh-oh." Jimmy poke me. "Look who's here."

Mrs. Williams! With her two little boys. They better not bother me today.

"Hey, B.J.!" Linda wave. "Come watch Lucky go in!"

She hold up a stick. "Okay, Lucky—fetch!"

She throw the stick in the shallow water. Lucky wade in before she even let go and bounce around looking for it. All of a sudden he duck under, come up with the stick in his mouth, and start to swim back. I have to laugh: he doing the real dog paddle! Nose in the air, front paws up under his chin. He wade in to Linda and drop the stick in front of her, shaking hisself off. His fur all slick down from the wet.

"Good, Lucky! You got it!" I look at Jim. "Want to—"

He staring out at the raft. Some kids fooling around out there. One, that look like a girl, wave.

"That's Peggy." He wave back. He look at me. "I'm just gonna go out and see her a minute, okay?"

"Sure." I watch him run down the beach and dive in. I like to cut through the water nice and smooth like him. He make it out to the raft in about two minutes.

"B.J.! *Watch!*" Linda hold the stick up over her head and throw it out. Lucky go after it but he can't find it. He swim around in a circle, barking.

"Over there, Lucky." I point to where the stick go in. Lucky scrabble around for a while, but then he give up and wade back without it.

"That's okay, Lucky." I reach out to pat him. "Hey!" He shake hisself off all over me! "You dumb dog, you get me all wet!"

Linda laugh. "He always does that. Come on, B.J., help me find a stick," she say. "He wants another chance."

I look around, but I don't see a good stick.

"Wait—I'll get one." Linda run up the beach.

Lucky jump around me, barking like he think I got the stick.

"I don't have it. See?" I show him my empty hands. "Come on, let's go play in the water plain."

I start to wade in and he wade in with me. He look cute with his hair plaster down. He look skinny, compare to when he dry.

"Hey, Lucky!" I splash water at him.

He bark like he laughing.

"Hey, Lucky!" Jimmy yell from the raft. "You having fun in the water?"

Lucky look around, barking. He don't know where Jimmy calling from.

"Out there, Lucky." I wave at the raft. "Look."

Uh-oh—soon as I raise my hand in the air Lucky hurl hisself at the water. He think I throw a stick out there. Hey—he swimming out to the deep!

"Lucky!" I yell.

He keep on going.

"Lucky—*stop!*" I wade out to my neck, after him.

But he keep on swimming. He must think the stick go out by the raft. Oh, man—he too *old* to swim way out there. He could drown!

I take a deep breath and dive in.

Breathe, stroke, breathe—I got to catch him! I pull myself through the water fast as I can, kicking my feet hard, raising up my head the way I been practicing. I see Lucky head, in front of me, raise up out of the water. Look like he paddling hard. But what if he sink down? What if *I* do? *Hang on*, I tell him in my mind. *Swim!*

I hear a yell and a splash. Somebody dive off the raft. I turn my face to look and water come in my nose. My arms starting to get tired. I bet Lucky little legs tired too. It look like he slowing down. Or else I'm gaining on him—oh, yeah, I think I'm getting closer! Just a little ways more . . . I close my eyes and try to concentrate on strokes and kicks. Breathe. Stroke. Breathe . . .

Somebody yelling. "Come on, Lucky! I got you!"

Jimmy! He right in front of me, holding on to Lucky collar.

"Come on, B.J.!" he yell. "You're almost at the raft!"

I have to stop and tread water a second to rest myself. I feel like I'm too beat to swim one more stroke. But then I do. Stroke, stroke . . . I raise my head up and look. The raft right in front of me, and Jimmy shoving Lucky up on it. He safe!

I grab a hold of the raft and heave myself halfway up. Peggy Holland lean down and pull me the rest of the way.

"You made it!" Jimmy yell from the water.

"Yeah." I just lay there. I'm too tired to talk. I reach out my hand and touch Lucky tail. He give a little bark and shake hisself off. My heart pounding so hard I can't hardly catch my breath. But who cares? I make it. I make it to the raft!

<hr />

"A-men."

The organ stop playing and we sit back down in a row: Norm, Jackie, Linda, me, Jimmy. We all so clean I can smell the soap.

The South Bridgeton church just like a church in a picture. White, with a pointy steeple, on top of a hill. Inside there wood benches in rows, a organ, flower on the altar, and windows all along the sides with the sun coming through.

I see Danny Carlson and his mother and little brothers sitting up front. Chris, Kenny, Peggy Holland—I bet I know just about all the people

in here, from out at the pond or around South
Bridgeton. I even see the preacher one time, outside the post office, only then she just look like a
regular person, with jeans and a little baby in a,
like, backpack.

Now she wearing a black robe and reading an-
nouncements from a notebook. Somebody back
from vacation, somebody sick in the hospital. A
bake sale for the day-care center, a meeting about
peace . . .

". . . welcome a special guest," I hear her say.

Jimmy kick my foot. She looking right at me! I
sit up fast.

". . . who's staying with the Roberts family—
B.J. Johnson, from New York City. We're happy
to have you with us, B.J." She smile. "I know
we'll all want to say hello—"

Everybody looking at me. I like to duck down
and hide, I'm so embarrass. I don't know if the
preacher expect me to say something back, or
what.

Then Buddy Carlson jump up in his seat.
"Hello, B.J.!" he call out.

Everybody laugh. I have to laugh too. I wave
at Buddy. Mrs. Carlson pull him back down and
give him a hug.

"That was a nice welcome, Buddy," the
preacher say. Then she read some more an-
nouncements, and we stand up and sing and the
church go on.

On the way out, people come and say hello. But they say it to all our family, not just to me. Most of them stop asking me if South Bridgeton look little after New York City. Today they all asking each other a new stupid question: "Is it hot enough for you?" Jimmy bet me we hear ten people say that after church. So far two people ask me.

At least I can say "A-yup" good now. I been practicing.

At the door, the preacher take my hand. "I hope we'll see you next Sunday, B.J."

Jackie shake her head. "No—" she say. "B.J. won't be here next Sunday." She look at me funny. "He's going home in three days."

Three *days!* That's the first time it really hits me. In three days, I'm going home.

11

"And now, ladies and gentlemen—the animal parade!"

The clown with a red wig blow on his trumpet. The girl in the top hat bang her drum. The judge—a lady in overalls and a straw hat—sitting on a high stool under a umbrella, and the audience standing in a circle on the grass. This the animal show at the fair, that Linda been practicing for.

The little kids start to come out of the barn with their animals: two dogs, two cats, a goat, a pig on a leash, a calf, a pony—hey, Linda! And old Sweetie strutting along behind her with a yellow ribbon around her neck.

"Yay, Linda!" we call. "Way to go, Sweetie!"

Me and Jimmy and Danny wave, but Linda don't wave back. She trying to act like a professional animal trainer. She train Sweetie to follow her around the yard by dribbling a trail of corn behind her.

Sweetie don't care where she at, back home or in a animal show, just so that corn fall down in front of her. She hop right along after Linda, clucking and bobbing her head and looking around with her bright little eyes.

All the audience must be families, because everybody calling out the same as us: "Hey, Ronny!" "Yay, Star!" "Melissa!" The little kids all dress up. Linda have yellow ribbons on her pigtails to match the one on Sweetie neck.

The animals suppose to come up to the judge so she can look them over, but some of them won't. One dog just lay on the grass and roll around. The goat won't even move, even when the boy pull his rope and the clown shove him from behind. But old Sweetie strut right up to the judge behind Linda like she think she the star of the show. The judge check her out real serious and write something down in a notebook.

"I hope she likes Sweetie the best," Jimmy say.

Me too. I want Linda to get a prize, she work so hard for it.

The judge take her time with each animal. Then she give the clown her notebook and he read out the awards.

"Best Groomed, Fluffy the Cat." The drummer bang the drum and the girl that own the cat run up for her ribbon.

The clown call out three more awards—Most Obedient, Friendliest, and Funniest—and the judge give out three more ribbons. You can tell what family go with each kid because they the ones that clap loudest. We just waiting. I'm holding my breath for Linda.

"Best Trained," the clown call out—"Sweetie the Chicken!"

Linda scoop Sweetie up in her arms and run to get her ribbon. We go wild. "Yay, Linda!" We slapping each other backs like our team win the World Series.

Then the drummer bang her drum and the clown turn a cartwheel, and the little kids and their animals parade back to the barn.

We go in the barn after them to congratulate Linda. Jackie pin the red ribbon to her shirt front. She look so proud! Sweetie proud too. She cluck and fluff up her feathers when we put her back in Wiggles old cage, that we bring her in. Linda give her fresh water, and we leave her there with Fluffy the Cat in a cage beside her. She probably sleep till we take her home.

The rest of the barn full of garden exhibits. All kind of vegetables—pumpkins, squash, corn, purple cabbage, potatoes that look like faces, turnips and carrots shape like people. I like the flower table best. The flowers so pretty all together. Roses, lilies, zinnias—

"Hey, Linda," I call. "Where your zinnias?"

She give me a funny look. "I forgot them."

Her flowers blooming good now. Great big ones—

orange, pink, red—I like to pick some for the table but Linda always say she saving them for the fair. Too bad she forget them, because I bet they win a prize—they big as any ones here.

"Look at all the jam people brought!" Jimmy checking out the preserve table. We bring our jam in here when we first come, and the table practically empty. Now it's full.

I count all the jars that say RASPBERRY. Sixteen! I shove our jar to the front so the judge be sure to see it.

Somebody heave up behind me. I swing around. Mrs. Williams! With a big jar of what look like raspberry jam. Oh, boy. *Seventeen.*

She slap it down on the table in front of ours. "Well, look who's here! I'm surprised you had time for jam, Jackie, all the extra work you've got this summer."

"Oh, the boys made the jam," Jackie say, quick. "I just helped pick the berries."

Mrs. Williams raise her eyes. "I could never get my boys to work around the kitchen." She sound like she proud of it. Well, too bad on her, if she too lazy to teach them.

"Boy, would I like to show her," Jimmy say when we go out of there. "I bet she'd be surprised if we win a ribbon!"

"Don't get your hopes up, hon," Jackie say. "All those jars of jam and there's only three prizes . . ."

Yeah, but we still could win one of them. Anyway,

we got a long time to wait before we find out. After the barbecue dinner, that's when they give out the ribbons.

Me and Jimmy and Danny go around the whole fair, checking out the booths. We try the ring toss and the dart board and the place where you suppose to throw clothespins in a bottle. We don't win no prizes, but it's still fun.

Then we buy a bag of homemade cookies and sit down on the grass and eat them and watch the people go by. I see a lot of people I know. The man from the Bridgeton Market come over and say hello. "You boys having a good time?"

We say, "A-yup."

"Let's go check out the rummage sale." Jimmy stand up. "Before all the good stuff's gone."

We duck around behind the booths to get out of people way. The pony ride back here. We stop and watch a man set a girl on a cute little shaggy-hair pony and lead her around the grass. I sort of like to go on the pony, but I don't say nothing. It look like just little kids doing it. Anyway, I rather ride on a real horse. Too bad I never get to, in the country. I could of, if Barbara sister get that horse, but she didn't. She might get a different one, but now it's too late for me.

We cut across the grass to the rope-off rummage sale place and go in.

I look around at all the tables pile with stuff: dishes, clothes, toys, blankets, car parts, pots and pans—plenty of people in New York like a chance to buy good use stuff like this. I guess country people must need it, too, because there a lot of them walking around the tables, holding things up, trying on coats and boots and shoes.

Danny go to look at a fishing pole. Me and Jimmy go over to look at the books.

I never see this many books except in a library. They got all kind. I pick one up: *Modern Typing.* Mama already know about that. I show Jimmy where it say "25¢" on the front page. "That all this book cost?"

"Yeah," he say. "They're always cheap at the rummage sale. Kids' books usually just cost ten cents. Want to go look at them?"

"Nah, I'm staying here." All these books, I bet I find some good presents to take home. I feel in my pocket where my money is. I got eight dollars—five from Daddy, plus the three Norm give each of us for the fair. He tell us, "You kids are gonna run me broke!" when he hand it out. But I know he just kidding.

It seem like there a book for just about anything you want to know! *Congress and the President. Heating with Wood Stoves. The Vietnam Years.* My daddy have a friend, Willard, that die in the Vietnam War. Hey— *Spanish for Beginners.* I ought to get this for myself. I already know some Spanish words. Luis, my friend that let me use his bike, teach me to read a subway ad for a roach trap: *Las cucarachas entran, pero no peuden salir.* That mean, "The cockroaches go in, but they can't go out." It sound a lot better in Spanish. I *am* gonna get me this book. Learn more words, surprise Luis when I go back home.

"Did you find something you want?" the lady behind the table ask.

"Yeah, this one." I hold it out and reach for my money.

"Never mind," she say. "I'll keep it for you. You can pay for everything later." She smile. "You look like the kind of boy who likes to read."

"Yeah." She right.

"Well, that's fine," she say.

I lift up a book and see a good one underneath it: *Martin Luther King, American Hero.* Oh, boy, I'm getting this for my daddy. Martin Luther King *his* hero. He use to have a Martin Luther King picture on the wall, only he take it with him when he move away. My daddy don't read that much, but I know he be proud if I give him this book.

The next table full of picture books. Real books, not baby ones. I pick up one call *Beautiful New Hampshire.* Pictures of mountains, farms, flowers—I bet Mama like to have this, see what the country look like. I'm getting it for her.

I show them to Jimmy. "Look what I got."

"Look what I got for you." He give me a book from behind his back. "I was going to save it for later, but I can't wait to show you."

It's *The Young Landlords!* "Hey, *thanks!*" Now I can

read the whole story when I go home. Show it to Leroy and Denise. I bet Mama like to read it too. She like funny stories. *"Thanks,* Jimmy," I say.

"Sure." He look please with hisself.

I know how he feel. It's good to find a present you sure somebody gonna like. I just find a good one for Linda—*Sammy the Seal,* by the same man that make *Danny and the Dinosaur.* Wait till she see it. I bet she be happy.

"Oh, my little boy used to love that book," the lady say when I go to pay her. "And I loved reading it to him, the story's so funny."

"Yeah," I say. "I just read *Danny and the Dinosaur* out loud. It's funny too."

"B.J.—" Danny call. "Come see all this stuff over here!" He slap a cowboy hat down on his head.

Me and Jimmy go where Danny is and start poking around the tables. I find a pair of work gloves that I know Norm need, because he spill oil on his other ones. And I get Jackie a flower pot with a chain that she can hang in a window.

But the best thing is what I find for Jimmy—a cute little flashlight, just about big as a pen, so he can still read in bed when he suppose to turn his light out. I just have to explain what it for in private, so Jackie don't hear.

All this stuff I buy only cost $5.65! I pay the man at the front table and drop the flashlight in my pocket before Jimmy see it. Then him and Danny and me go

out of the rummage sale and cut back across the fair-
grounds to the barbecue place, where men turning
chickens on a great big grill and lifting them off onto
plates.

We stand in line to get our dinners—chicken, po-
tato salad, cole slaw, bake beans, and pie. I take raspberry pie. That's my best kind. Then we carry our
food down the row of tables to where our families sitting, and squeeze in. Norm and Jackie and Linda and
Mrs. Carlson and the little boys and us fill up the
whole table.

It look like just about everybody at the fair come to
eat at the barbecue, and they all laughing and waving across the tables. A lot of people come over to talk
to Norm and Jackie and Mrs. Carlson. I guess everybody know them.

"Hey, Jimmy—there's your girlfriend." Danny
poke him.

Peggy Holland waving at us from her table. Me
and Danny wave back. Jimmy act like he too busy
eating but I bet he the first one over there when we
finish.

"Ladies and gentlemen—" A lady step up to a mi-
crophone. "It's time to give out the prizes for the best
entries in our wonderful exhibits."

Jimmy kick me. I sit up and try to look cool, but I
cross my fingers under the table.

"We've got a lot of prizes to give out," the lady go

on. "I hope you'll all bear with me while I read the list."

They must be a hundred prizes! The lady call out names and give out ribbons for vegetables, flowers, cake and pie, white bread, wheat bread, rye bread, zucchini bread—it seem like she never get to the jam. Linda and the little boys scramble down from the table and run off to play on the grass.

I watch them chase around. I rather go over there, too, instead of sit here all night and wait.

Just then, the lady call out, "Raspberry jam—"

Uh-oh! I sit up. I try not to look at Jimmy.

"First prize, Mary Widmer."

"Here!" A lady across from us jump up and run to get her ribbon.

I clap, to be polite.

"Second prize—Jeanette Williams."

I catch myself before I say a curse. Jimmy kick me—I bet he thinking the same thing! Mrs. Williams squeeze between the tables and go to the front for her red ribbon. She come back waving it in the air.

Jackie looking at me, so I clap. Not hard.

"And the third prize—" The lady check her list. "We seem to have *two* winners for this one—"

Hey!

"B.J. Johnson," she call out. "And Jimmy Roberts."

All right!

"Come on!" Jimmy pull me up and we run down the aisle to the judge. She hand us each a white ribbon and shake our hands. "Congratulations, boys."

We say, "Thanks!"

When we go back to our table, I sneak a look over to Mrs. Williams. She clapping hard, but she have a funny smile on her face, like she surprise.

Danny jump up and slap our backs, and Norm and Jackie and Mrs. Carlson all say, "Congratulations!" Linda and the little boys run up to see our ribbons. They say THIRD PRIZE in gold letters. Jimmy and me pin the ribbons to our shirts. We look at each other and laugh, we feeling so good.

After the barbecue, a lot of people come up and congratulate us. Peggy Holland so excited she just about knock Jimmy down, looking at his ribbon. She with two other girls I see at the pond.

"The band concert's going to start in a minute," one of them say. "Come on, let's go find a good place."

"Can we, Mom?" Jimmy ask.

"Yes, but stick around near the bandstand when it's over," she say, "so I can find you."

The lights around the bandstand go on and the band start to play. They not bad, for a country group. Loud. Peggy Holland and the other girls duck around to the back of the bandstand so we follow them. Some teenage kids back there, dancing. They all right. Peggy Holland grab Jimmy and try to make

him dance, but he won't, so I do. Jimmy look surprise. I guess I never tell him I can dance. There a lot
of things he don't know about me.

We all have a good time back of the bandstand.
Ken and Chris come by and we hang around after
the concert over, till Jackie come get us. Then we say
good night to Danny and his brothers and Mrs. Carlson. The little boys grab on to Norm like they not
letting him go. Norm lift each one up in the air and
shake him till he start to laugh, and set him down. I
know why they so crazy about Norm—they don't
have no daddy. Jimmy tell me last night. Last year,
Mr. Carlson get a divorce and go live in Florida. I feel
sorry for the little boys. Danny, too.

We get Sweetie from the barn and walk to our car.
Jackie sit up front with Norm, and the kids sit in
back, with Sweetie in her cage on the floor.

Jimmy roll down his window and stick his head
out. "I need air." He act like he choking. "Old
Sweetie stinks!"

"Don't mind him." Linda pat the cage. "He's just
jealous because you won a prize for Best Trained. *He*
would never win that!"

"You know what ribbon she should have won?"
Jimmy laugh. "The *P.U.* ribbon!"

"*Jimmy!*" Linda can't help laughing too.

Sweetie give a little cluck inside her cage, fluff her
feathers, and stick her head back under her wing. I
don't mind her smell that much. It's just a country

smell. Anyway, the air blowing through the windows nice and fresh.

Jimmy lean back on the seat. "Man, I am stuff! I shouldn't of eat all that pie."

"Me, neither." I look over at him. It's funny—Jimmy don't look nothing like Leroy, but sometimes he remind me of him.

I lay my head on the window edge and look out. I can just make out the trees in the fields, and the row of dark mountains behind them.

Jackie point. "Look, there's the first star." I look out her window where the sky still green from the last light. A bright star shining there.

"Star light," Linda say fast, "star bright, first star I see tonight, wish I may, wish I might—"

"Have the wish I wish tonight!" Jimmy and me finish up with her.

Jackie turn around. "Know what Norm and I wish?"

We hold our breath in the dark. Nobody want to break the spell.

She looking at me. "We wish B.J. would come back and stay with us next summer."

"Yay!" Linda yell so loud that Sweetie wake up and start clucking.

"That's just what *I* wished!" Jimmy slap me.

"Me too!" I slap him back. "Remember when we were camping? That's what I wish for, way back then!"

"Me *too!*"

"All of us wishing the same thing, that's bound to make it come true." Norm turn around and smile at us.

Then he shift down and speed up and we drive on home in the night.

The corn get ripe!

This how you eat corn in the country:

First, put a big pot of water on the stove to get hot. Set the table, so when the corn ready, you ready to eat it. Put butter, salt, and a lot of paper napkins on the table.

Then go pick the corn. You can tell the corn almost ripe when the ears get big, and the silky stuff on top, the tassels, turn dark-color and flop down. But if you not sure, pull down the husk a little ways and see if the good kernels come all the way up to the top. Then poke your nail in one kernel. If, like, cream come out, you know the corn ripe. If it's not, pull the husk back up and leave it.

Break the good ears off the stalk. When you got enough, bring them in the kitchen and lay them on newspapers. Make sure the water boiling. Call everybody to get ready to eat. Then shuck the corn—peel the husks back all the way and pull them off. Pick off all the little silky hairs. If you see a worm, pick it off too. Wrap up the corn trash in the papers and put it out the back door.

Drop the corn ears in the pot. Cook them about four minutes—not too long, or they get tough. Take the ears from the pot with tongs. Put them on a platter. Pass it around. Look out when you grab one. They *hot.*

There two ways to butter corn. One, spread butter on it with a knife. Two, put butter on your plate and rub the corn around in it. Whichever way you do, butter run off when you lift up the ear. That's why you need the napkins.

Eat. Some people eat corn around and around—one end, then the middle, then the other end. Other people eat like they playing a harmonica; eat a couple rows all the way to the end, then go back and start down again. Any way you eat it, corn taste so good you want to eat more.

So then, put more corn in the pot and start over. Most people usually eat two, three ears and stop, but I know two kids in New Hampshire (J.R. and B.J.J.) that one time eat six ears each.

When you eat all you *can* eat, take the corn trash—all the husks, silk, and cobs—and throw it on the compost heap to make good rich soil for next year corn to grow in.

Corn taste good, plus it's good for you. But eat too much and you be sorry. Only, you know you probably do the exact same thing next time, because fresh corn the best food in the world.

12

"Did you get the veggies?"

Jackie come out the back door with her pocketbook on her shoulder and my bag in her hand. She wearing the exact same check shirt she had on when I come. I can't hardly remember how she look to me back then, before I get to know her.

"I put them in the car," I say. Me and Jimmy pick my vegetables for home soon as we get up this morning. Carrots, peppers, cucumbers, a cabbage, five big tomatoes, and a whole lot of zucchini. One of them a giant I'm bringing to give Leroy. I bet he be surprise.

"They're going to get *hot* in there, all the way to Claremont." Jackie look at me like it my fault. "And then the whole long bus ride to the city . . ."

"They'll be okay." Norm come out with his camera. He take a lot of pictures the last couple days. He gonna send them to me and Mama. "The bus is air-conditioned, right, B.J.?"

"I guess so." I don't really remember, it's so long since I ride up on it.

"C'mon." Jimmy pull my arm. "You have to say good-bye to Wiggles."

"Well, be quick." Jackie head for the house. "You hear me, Jim? B.J.?" She sound like she mad at us, but I think she just sad because I'm going home. "And don't you kids let that rabbit loose, just when we're trying to get out of here. *Linda!*" she call. "Get down here, fast!"

Wiggles sitting at his new front door, like he waiting for me to come.

I poke my fingers in and touch his pink nose. "Hey, Wiggles. How you doing?"

Wiggles *wiggle* all over, he so glad to see me. I unlatch the door.

"Get his food, okay?" I tell Jimmy. "I just want to hold him a second." I take him out and hold him in my arms. His fur so *soft*. I lay my face in it. "You gonna miss me when I go?"

Wiggles shove his little feet against my chest. His little round shit fall down on my sneaker. I don't care. People might think it's disgusting, if they never live around animals. But it's just natural.

Jimmy set Wiggles food dish in the cage. "You better put him back in. We have to go."

I give Wiggles one last squeeze, shove him in with his food, and lock the door shut. "So long, Wiggles." I don't look back when we walk away. I wonder if rabbits know how to feel sad.

Norm call to us. "Go stand over there, guys, by the tree. I want a shot of you together." He look in his camera. "That's good—stay just like that. Okay—smile!"

I stand up straight. Jimmy stand up straight beside me. The sun shining in my eyes. I can't make myself smile.

Jimmy poke me. "Red Sox!"

I laugh. "Yankees!"

Norm snap. "Stay there!" He snap again. *"Jackie,"* he call. *"Linda!* Come get in the picture."

"I'm coming." Jackie run out of the house with my hat. "Look what you almost forgot." She shove it down on my head.

"Thanks." It's good she find it—I got to wear it on the bus. "Hey!" I look up. "Here come Lucky, to be in the picture!"

I already tell him good-bye upstairs. He lay on the bed next to my suitcase and watch me pack. I know he gonna miss me. When I lay down to pet him the last time, he lick my face and, like, whimper.

Jimmy haul Lucky over to the tree.

"Where's Linda?" Norm look around. "I want to get the whole family in this one. *Linda!"*

"Just a second," Linda call from the garden. "I'm coming."

"Linda, hurry!" Jackie look at her watch. "We're never going to make it, at this rate."

Linda come out through the corn with a big bunch

of flowers in her hand. She run up and shove them at me. "Here."

I look down. My arms full of flowers! Daisies, sweet peas, nasturtiums, zinnias. Hey—her best zinnias she never pick for the fair!

"What you want to pick your zinnias for?" I ask her.

"For you," she say, shy. "For a going-home present."

"Thanks!" I reach around the flowers and pull her pigtail. "They nice, Linda. They so pretty!" I just about choke up. She save her zinnias for *me!* She some sweet little kid.

"Hold the flowers up, B.J." Norm take a picture of me with Linda. "Now all of you." He make me and Jimmy kneel down with Lucky, and Jackie and Linda stand in back. Then he snap us two times.

"Well," he say. "I guess that's about it—"

"Wait!" Jackie grab the camera away, pull him over to us, and take our picture with him. "C'mon, folks. Let's see you smile."

My smile feel like it's stuck on my face.

Jackie snap again.

"How's B.J. going to carry those flowers all the way to New York?" Jimmy ask. "They'll just wilt on the bus."

I been thinking the same thing, but I don't like to say it.

Linda look like she gonna cry.

"No, they won't!" Jackie say quick. She take the flowers from me. "I'll cover the stems with wet paper towels and put them in a plastic bag and wrap newspaper around the whole bunch. When B.J. gets home, he can cut a little off the stems and put them in fresh water. They'll be fine."

She start up the steps again. "Don't just stand there," she call over her shoulder. "Go on, get in the car. I'll be right out. Come *on*, Lucky." She shove him in the door.

That's the last time I see him, till next summer. I bet he know I'm coming back. I bet he be glad when I do.

Jimmy tap Linda shoulder. "Where you want to sit?"

"In back, next to B.J."

"Go on then." He fold up the seat so she can climb in. "Push over—let B.J. sit in the middle."

Linda push over. I get in and Jimmy come after me. That's the first time since I come that we just get in the car without a argument. The last time, too.

Norm look at my bag. "You get plenty of vegetables for your mom?"

"Yeah." I wonder if Mama making something special for when I come home. Fry chicken or something. I bet she rushing around to get ready to go meet my bus. I be glad to look out the bus window, see her standing there waiting for me.

Jackie run out with the flowers wrap in newspaper.

She get in the car and slam the door shut. Then she look around. "You all ready, B.J.?"

"Yeah." At least my stuff is. I got so much to take home! Flowers, veggies, new clothes, raspberry jam, my prize ribbon, applesauce from Jackie for Mama, birch bark, the Spanish book, my books for Mama and Daddy. Oh, yeah, and my *Young Landlords* book. Leroy and Denise go crazy when I lend it to them!

Norm start the car, back it up, and turn around.

I look hard at everything so I don't forget: barn, garden, back steps—I lean over so I can see up to my window. *So long, house. So long, Lucky.* I bet he sleeping up on my bed.

Norm drive into the street. I look back till we turn and I can't see our house no more. Now I know I'm on my way, but I still can't make myself believe it. It's hard to think of yourself in some other place, when you still in the place where you at.

"B.J.!" Linda go. "You forgot to say good-bye to the chickens!"

Jimmy laugh. "What did you want him to do, kiss them?" He smack kisses in the air. "Good-bye, darling Charm, good-bye, Princess, oh, my sweet little Sweetie, how can I ever leave you?"

I have to smile, he so ridiculous. I bet I do miss the chickens, though. Flapping around you when you open the door, cackling when they lay a egg.

"Want me to tell them you said good-bye?" Linda ask.

"Sure, you tell them." I don't care if Jimmy laugh. I like to make Linda feel good. "Tell them I'm gonna miss the nice fresh eggs."

"There's Danny!" Linda say.

"Danny!" Jimmy yell out the window. "We're taking B.J. to the bus!"

Norm pull over and Danny ride up. He stick his head in the window. "You going *now?*"

"Yeah."

"Well, so long!" He reach in and slap me. "See you next summer."

"Yeah, see you." I slap him back. "Say good-bye to—"

But Danny take off, zoom up to his house. When we drive by, he come out on the porch with one of his little brothers—hey, there come his mother and his other brother. They all waving.

"Bye, B.J.!" they call. "Bye!"

"Bye!" I wave back till we turn.

We go past the school. "I can't believe I'm going back to school in two weeks," Jimmy say.

"Me, neither." But I don't mind. I be glad to see all the kids again. Tell them about the country.

We go on past the church, post office, store. I try to look at everything. That's my last time I see South Bridgeton for a whole year.

"Here comes the pond," Jimmy say. "Hey—somebody's out on the raft."

"Maybe Peggy." Boy, I like to swim out to the raft just one more time.

"I bet you can't wait to tell your mom about swimming," Jackie say.

All of a sudden Linda grab my hand. *"Don't go home, B.J.! Stay here forever!"*

"Linda!" Jackie turn around and frown at her. "Don't start that, now. It won't make things any easier." She look at me like she memorizing my face. "Be glad for all the fun we've had with B.J.," she say. "And think of the good times we'll have next year."

"Yeah, wait till next year," Jimmy say. "That's going to be so cool, B.J."

"I know it." Next year a long way off, though.

"And we can write to B.J. in the meantime," Jackie tell Linda.

"Yeah—know what, B.J.?" Linda say. "I'm writing you my first letter, when I learn how to write in school! I already know how to write your name—just put *B* and *J!*"

"That's right," I say. "I be waiting for your letter, you hear?" Before, I never get no mail in my box. Now I bet I get a lot, cause I'm gonna write a lot of letters, all winter.

We come to the outside of Claremont already. Norm steer around a van. "Seems like the traffic gets worse every day."

"Well, there's good reason for it," Jackie say. "All the Fresh Air families coming to town—that's a lot of excitement for this part of New Hampshire." She don't look excited, though. She look sad.

We drive into town, go around the square, and

turn at a corner I remember from when I come, where Jackie show me a apartment house. Then we stop at a traffic light and I see the school and the parking lot where our bus come before. Some people already there, but I don't see no bus.

Linda lean out. "The bus isn't there. Maybe it's not coming. Maybe this is the wrong day."

Jimmy say, "Why would all those people be there, dummy, if it's the wrong day?"

"I don't know." She bite her pigtail.

"The bus is probably just late or something," Jimmy say, in a nice way. "It has to come, Linda. But then next summer, it's going to bring B.J. back."

Linda give him a little smile.

Norm drive across the street and park by some other cars in front of the school. "Well." He turn off the engine. "Here we are."

I look out. Just for a minute, I wish it *was* the wrong day. Get use to a place, you feel funny to go away from it.

"Well." Now Jackie say it. "Here we are."

I hear a fly in the car somewhere. Buzzing.

We sit there.

"Well, we can't just sit here." Jackie open her door and jump out with my flowers.

Then we all get out. Norm take my stuff out of the trunk. Jimmy pick up my suitcase and Linda grab my bag. We start to go where the people are. I walk between Norm and Jackie. They each put a arm around me. We walk slow.

Kids are running around the schoolyard, playing tag. Some of them I remember from the bus. I guess the other kids from the families they stay with.

Somebody run up behind me and slap my leg.

I wheel around. It's the little kid that suck his thumb when we come. Now he laughing. He hold up a stuff rabbit almost as big as he is and show me.

"Hey, how ya doing!" I slap his hand.

A girl run over and scoop him up with his rabbit. She look at me. "Is that your friend, Bobby?" she ask the boy.

He nod his head. Then he wiggle out of her arms and run over to a man and lady. They catch him. I bet he have a good time up here. He look more happy than when he come.

The lady walk over and say hello to us. "What's your name, dear?" she ask me.

"B.J." I hope she not going to ask a Mrs. Williams question.

"Well, B.J., could we ask you a favor?" she say. "Just, you know, to look out for Bobby on the bus?" She sort of laugh. "I know Mrs. Anderson will be riding with you. But still—"

The man come up with Bobby hanging on to his hand. "He might be more worried than he lets on," he say low, so Bobby can't hear. "About finding his mother when the bus gets to New York. If you could just talk to him along the way . . ."

"Sure." I know a little kid might worry about that. "Hey, Bobby, you want to sit with me on the bus?" I ask him. I don't mind—Sondra and Celeste can sit near us. "You and me gonna stick together, okay?"

"Yeah." He have a cute little smile.

"Thank you, B.J." The lady look at me like I'm a hero or something.

"B.J.—come on!" Jimmy call. He setting my suitcase on the pile.

"See you on the bus," I tell Bobby.

Jackie smile at the woman. "He'll be fine," she say. "They all will." She wipe her face on her sleeve. "This heat's something fierce."

I bet it's hot in New York, too.

Linda grab my hand. "When's the bus coming?"

Jackie look at her watch. "It's due any minute. Anything you want to tell B.J., you better tell him now."

Jimmy come up and poke me. "I want to tell him the Red Sox are the best!"

"Yeah?" I poke him back. "I want to tell you you crazy!"

"Say what?" He jump me and we fall down on the grass, laughing.

"Come on, guys." Norm pull us up. "You're dressed too nice for that kind of stuff." He brush off my hat and set it back on my head.

"What's B.J.'s mother going to think of us if he comes home all dirty?" Jackie pull me to her. "Oh, B.J.," she whisper in my ear. "Be sure and tell your mom how much we thank her for sharing you with us!" She fix my hat that Norm just fix. "You're going to write us like you promised, right? Let us know how you're doing—"

Uh-oh. I hear a honk.

People start to yell. "The bus!"

We watch the bus heave up the street, turn in the driveway, and roll to a stop by the suitcases.

"B.J., c'mon—hurry up and get a good seat!" Jimmy pull me over.

Norm lift Linda on his shoulder, and we all head for the bus. I look back for Bobby.

"I'll get our seat!" I call to him.

Everybody crowd up to the door. The bus driver open it and get out. Hey—he the same one that bring us! He look around and wave like he glad to see us again.

Mrs. Anderson go up and talk to him for a minute. Then she stand on a step, shade her eyes, and look out at us.

"Time to load up," she say. "Let's get these kids on the bus."

Then everybody start hugging.

Jackie put her arm around me. "B.J.—"

"*B.J.!*"

I turn around. Hey, Celeste! And Sondra, and Wesley and Joyce and the baby!

"Hey!" I wave back. Oh, boy, I'm glad to see them! Me and the girls can sit together all the way home, have us some fun.

"Save us a seat!" Celeste call.

"Yeah!" I look around for Bobby. His family hugging him. He not smiling now.

Jackie grab me, hard. "Bye, hon." She shove my flowers at me. She crying. "Don't forget us, now. We'll be waiting till you come back."

"Me too." I reach up and kiss her cheek. "Goodbye, Jackie." I can't hardly believe I didn't know her just two weeks ago. Now she like my next mother.

"B.J.!" Linda scramble down from Norm's shoulder and grab me around the neck.

I hug her. "Bye, Linda. You take it easy now, okay?" I can't hardly look at her, she so sad. "Thanks for the zinnias," I tell her. "They blue-ribbon flowers."

She try to smile. People crowd up around us. Norm grab me and hold me close. "Good luck, son."

"Yeah." I look up at him. I see tears in his eyes. I can feel tears in my eyes. I put my arms around him. "So long, Norm."

"Write to us, now." He pat my back. "Let us know how you're doing."

"I will." That's the first thing I'm gonna do when I get home, buy me a New York City postcard and send it to them, so they know I get there safe.

"Let's go, folks!" Mrs. Anderson call out.

"Jimmy!" I got to say good-bye to my friend.

"B.J.!" He slap me five. "See you next summer!"

I slap him back. "Yeah, man. I be here."

Then we just stand there. I like to say something, only I don't know what. "Yankees!" I go.

Jimmy say, "Red Sox!" But he not laughing.

I like to say some other things, but everybody start to move and we get shove apart.

I turn around. I got to find Bobby. *There* he is. His family push him up to me.

"Hey, man." I grab his hand. "You ready to go?"

We almost at the bus steps. "Say so long to your folks," I tell him. "Come on, they want to see you wave."

He turn around and wave.

I look out in the crowd for my family. I see them— Norm, Jackie, Linda, and old Jimmy, yelling at me.

"So long, B.J.!"

They all waving.

I wave. Oh, man, I'm gonna miss them.

Somebody whack me on the back.

"Ow!" I look around.

Terrence!

"Hey, man!" I help Bobby up the steps in front of me. I'm surprise, but I'm glad to see old Terrence. Wait till I tell him all I do up here!

"Guess what, Terrence? You ever swim way out to a—"

Somebody shove me in the bus. I put my arm around Bobby and head him to the back. We can all sit together—him and me, Sondra and Celeste, and Terrence, too. Talk about the country. Talk about New York. I can't believe we be there today!

Hey, wait till this old bus zoom down Broadway. Wait till we hit the terminal, see all the people waiting for us. Wait till Mama see me! Wait till I go find Leroy, tell him about the country. Wait till I see Denise!

Oh, man. All of a sudden, I can't wait to be home!

BETTY MILES is the author of many popular novels for young readers, among them *The Real Me, Maudie and Me and the Dirty Book,* and *The Trouble with Thirteen.* She has taught and written about children's literature and was an editor of the Bank Street Readers. She frequently visits schools around the country to talk about books with students, teachers, librarians, and parents. Ms. Miles lives with her husband in Tappan, New York. They are the parents of three grown children.